I0599164

THE COMPLETE CASES OF
MARIANO MERCADO, VOLUME 2

**BOOKS IN THE DIME DETECTIVE
UNIFORM EDITION LIBRARY:**

The Complete Cases of the Acme Indemnity Op, Volume 2 by Jan Dana

The Complete Cases of Colonel Kaspir, Volume 1 by C.P. Donnel, Jr.

The Complete Cases of Jeffery Wren, Volume 2 by G.T. Fleming-Roberts

The Complete Cases of John Wade, Volume 1 by William R. Cox

The Complete Cases of Mariano Mercado, Volume 2 by D.L. Champion

The Complete Cases of Mr. Maddox, Volume 3 by T.T. Flynn

THE COMPLETE CASES OF

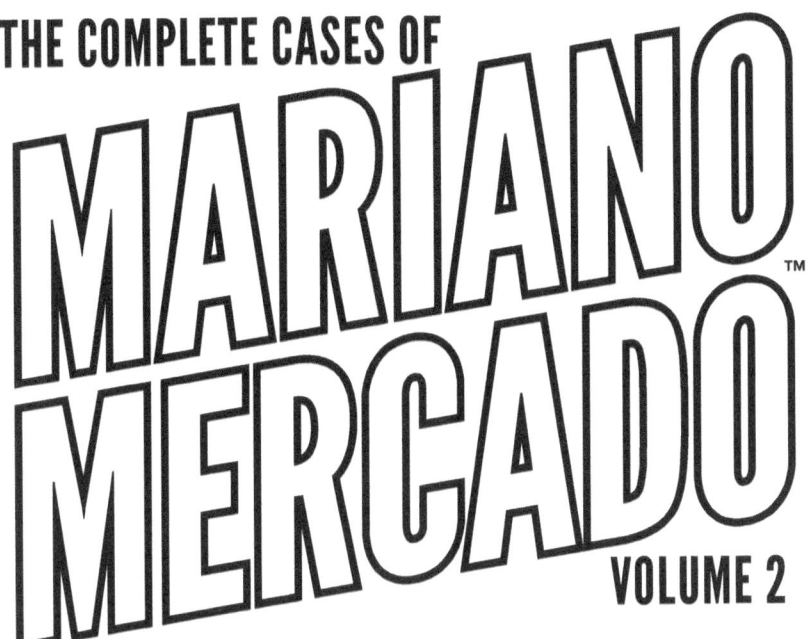

MARIANO MERCADO™

VOLUME 2

D.L. CHAMPION

INTRODUCTION BY
JOHN WOOLEY

ILLUSTRATIONS BY
JOHN FLEMING GOULD

POPULAR PUBLICATIONS • 2024

© 2024 Popular Publications, an imprint of Steeger Properties, LLC

First Edition—2024

PUBLISHING HISTORY

"No Place Like Homicide" originally appeared in the April 1946 issue of *Dime Detective* magazine. Copyright 1946 by Popular Publications, Inc. Copyright renewed 1974 and assigned to Steeger Properties, LLC. All rights reserved.

"A Hound for Murder" originally appeared in the December 1946 issue of *Dime Detective* magazine. Copyright 1946 by Popular Publications, Inc. Copyright renewed 1974 and assigned to Steeger Properties, LLC. All rights reserved.

"Suitable for Framing" originally appeared in the May 1947 issue of *Dime Detective* magazine. Copyright 1947 by Popular Publications, Inc. Copyright renewed 1975 and assigned to Steeger Properties, LLC. All rights reserved.

"The Shabby Shroud" originally appeared in the June 1948 issue of *Dime Detective* magazine. Copyright 1948 by Popular Publications, Inc. Copyright renewed 1976 and assigned to Steeger Properties, LLC. All rights reserved.

ALL RIGHTS RESERVED

No part of this book may be reproduced or utilized in any form or by any means, electronic or mechanical, without permission in writing from the publisher.

This edition has been marked via subtle changes, so anyone who reprints from this collection is committing a violation of copyright.

"Mariano Mercado" and "Dime Detective" are trademarks of Steeger Properties, LLC.

TABLE OF CONTENTS

MARIANO MERCADO'S CHAMPION
BY JOHN WOOLEY

THE **SYNDICATED** obituary, which ran in a number of newspapers across the country during the weekend of March 22–24, 1968, was nothing if not succinct. Appearing under the headline " 'PHANTOM' WRITER DIES" in many papers, and carrying a New York dateline, it read, *in toto:* "D'Arcy Lyndon Champion, 65, a writer under the name of D.L. Champion, died Friday [March 22] in a hospital here. Champion originated 'The Phantom Detective,' which ran in the magazine of that name and was later serialized on radio."

That was it. No mention of any other in the panoply of characters who'd leapt from his typewriter over the preceding decades; just an acknowledgement of a pulp-magazine hero he'd created, or at least helped create, 35 years earlier. (For a fuller explanation of Champion's connection to the character, check out Ed Hulse's introduction to Steeger Books' *The Complete Cases of Inspector Allhoff, Vol. 1.*)

While there's no doubt that the Phantom Detective certainly deserves enshrinement as one of the very first and longest-lasting of the pulpwood heroes, Champion—who left the stable of PD authors after a couple of years—hardly built his fiction career on that title alone. For about two decades, until the death of the pulps in the early '50s, he introduced a number of different series characters, most notably a trio of offbeat crimefighters that ran in Popular Publications' two most prestigious detective-story titles: *Black Mask* and *Dime Detective.* They were, in order, the "legless coffee drunkard" (as he was sometimes described), Inspector Allhoff, who began in the July 1938 *Dime Detective;* Rex Sackler, "the parsimonious prince of penny-pinchers," who debuted in the July 1, 1939 number of *Detective Fiction Weekly,* moving over to *Black Mask* in July of 1940; and the subject of this volume, Mexico City-based Mariano Mercado, "the germ-free dick," whose adventures began in the September 1944 issue of *Dime Detective*—some 58 years before a similarly germophobic detective named Monk debuted on the USA Network.

Beyond the memorable taglines that described them, these three Champion creations have a couple of things in common. First, all of their stories are narrated by a secondary character, in the Holmes-Watson/Nero Wolfe-Archie Goodwin tradition. Second, each of them is, charitably, quite eccentric, same as in the Wolfe and, arguably to a lesser extent, the Holmes tales.

Maybe that's only right. Based on the research we've done, a pretty good case can be made for their creator being more than a little offbeat himself.

BORN IN the Australian town of Caulfield, Victoria, a suburb of Sydney, on August 12, 1902, D'Arcy Lyndon Champion, along with his parents, arrived in San Francisco via steamship almost exactly a year later. Both his mother, Lyda, and his father, Thomas, were natives of Britain, and while Thomas apparently had been a lawyer, by the time the 1920 census rolled around, he listed his occupation as "Assistant Manager, Theatrical Club." (Theatrical clubs— the best-known being the still-extant Lambs—were social organizations for people in the performing arts.) Meanwhile, Thomas's 19-year-old son was listed in the census as Darcy L. Champion, his business as "Actor, Theater." All three Champions were living together in Manhattan at the time.

Right off the bat, things become a little muddled with regards to Champion fils' career. First of all, while he was listed in the census as a stage actor, he's not in the Internet Broadway Database (IBDB) as either D'Arcy Champion or Jack D'Arcy, a name he began using in the early '20s. On one occasion, a Brooklyn newspaper announced Jack D'Arcy as a cast member in a 1930 Broadway play called Room 349; in fact, that was an actor named Roy D'Arcy, who had a pretty good career as a silent-screen villain.

Where we do run into Jack D'Arcy early on is in the newspapers; specifically, in a syndicated column called "The Conning Tower," presided over by a famed columnist named Franklin P. Adams. Often referred to by only his initials, F.P.A. was a member of the Algonquin Round Table, that noteworthy group of writers and others who met regularly to exchange observations and witticisms at New York's Algonquin Hotel throughout the 1920s. He published work, usually poetry, by several of his round-table compadres—including Dorothy Parker and Robert Benchley—in "The Conning Tower."

At least twice, the column also featured contributions of light verse from a young writer named Jack D'Arcy. The first, titled "The Conservative Shepherd to His Love," finds the poet asking his love where he stands with her. The concluding four lines provide a cynically humorous twist:

> If with you I'm not a winner,
>   That means little in my life.
>   I'll buy you a farewell dinner
>   And take you home to meet the wife.

That one was published in newspapers around the country on April 16, 1923, when Champion/D'Arcy was 20. About a month later, on May 21, came another, "Plaint of the Literal Vaudevillian to His Agent," which more closely reflected its author's milieu.

> I long to sing a chantry of some ivy-covered chantry
> Where the blue grass and the cotton blossoms grow.
>> To murmur low some sonnet of a tree with peaches on it
>> Or to carol of the Suwanne River's flow.
> I crave to chant a lyric, an adoring panegyric,
>> Of Annabelle, who kissed me in the lane;
> My dream's to sing of mother in some southern state or other.
>> But the whole confounded family lives in Maine.

While appearances in "The Conning Tower" could kick-start writing careers, as it did with both Parker and James Thurber, nothing like that happened with Champion. But the very fact that he made the column at all indicates that he was at least around the New York creative scene in the early '20s; it's not outside the realm of possibility, for instance, that his dad's theatrical club gave young Champion access to personalities like F.P.A. and, say, the prominent actress Greta Nissen.

From the August 23, 1928 issue of *The Miami News*, datelined New York: "For driving too fast in a car with Greta Nissen of the stage and screen, Jack D'Arcy, artist, is in the hoosegow. He was fined $25 and had the wherewithal, but, as Miss Nissen explains: 'Mr. D'Arcy does not want to be set free. He wants the experience. You see, he's never been in jail before.'"

So for those of you keeping score, in the '20s Champion listed his occupation as actor, was described in print as an artist, and was published as a poet. He seems to have been one of those insouciant, devil-may-care, young Jazz Age dabblers, a target demographic for H.L. Mencken and George Jean Nathan's *The Smart Set*.

Then, somewhere in the late '20s, Champion jumped into the pulps. Perhaps it was because he'd gotten married in 1926—to a woman of Irish extraction from Virginia named Ann—and found it imperative to become a bread-winner. The two had a daughter, Joan, as well. Her birth, around the time they tied the knot, undoubtedly added to the financial urgency.

There may have been other reasons involved in his turn-ing to the all-fiction pulpwood magazines for a livelihood. But whatever his motivation, he would become very good at what he did.

ACCORDING TO John Locke's detailed Cham-pion biography in Volume Two of *Ghost Stories: The Maga-zine and Its Makers* (Off-Trail Publications, 2010), the first evidence we have of Champion's entry into the periodical business comes from the legendary Walter Gibson, who was editing a publication called *Tales of Magic and Mystery* in the late '20s. Gibson, wrote Locke, described Champion as his associate editor on that short-lived effort. Before the decade was over, Champion would branch out into fiction writing, hitting three different pulps—*Flying Aces, Flight,* and *Gangster Stories*—under a second pseudonym, Tom Champion, perhaps a nod to his father.

Whether the name under the title was Tom Cham-pion or Jack D'Arcy, the '30s saw Champion become entrenched as a wordsmith for several publishers. In 1933, under the house name of G. Wayman-Jones, he wrote the very first Phantom Detective novel, "The Emperor of Death" (February 1933); as we've seen, that would be the only character cited in his syndicated obit. (The piece used the term "originated" to describe Champion's involvement with the *Phantom Detective*. In his *Ghost Stories* bio, Locke, paraphrasing editor Jack Schiff, wrote that "Champion helped create the character in conjunction with [chief editor] Leo Margulies and others.")

People who knew and worked with him during that time recall a man who definitely had his idiosyncrasies. Veteran fictioneer Frank Gruber, for instance, told pulp aficionado Lynn Hickman in a 1968 letter that Champion was "a real character" and "a big night club man," while Locke quotes Schiff as saying, re: Champion's work on *Phantom Detective*, "One of the troubles was that he sometimes was not responsible. So we had to have backups. It was a question of self-preservation. Jack used to be quite a drinker. We had to be sure we could put out an issue. And he might be off on a bender."

While *The Phantom Detective* magazine gave Champion plenty of work for a couple of years, and he continued to hit other pulp markets as well—usually under the Jack D'Arcy name—there's evidence that he, like many others of his ilk, was trying to hack his way out of the pulp jungle into the better-paying, more prestigious slick magazines of the time. A couple of lines in "The Pony Express" section of the April 4, 1935, *Writer's Review* may have indicated his frustration with those efforts: "[Jack] D'Arcy wonders why more people don't start writing for the slicks. 'They might just as well starve writing for the slicks as starve writing for the pulps,' he caustics...."

It's also possible that his attempts to break into the slick-paper magazines account for his slim publication credits in the year 1937. He made only two known appearances in the pulps that year, although he also had a vignette in the December 25 issue of the slick *Collier's,* as well as one in the January 8, 1938 issue of the same magazine. They may have been the tip of the iceberg, with many more of his slicks-aimed stories submerged in an ocean of rejection slips.

The *Collier's* shorts, however, do mark a turning point in his career. According to the Fiction Mags Index, they are his first two stories published under his given name. With a couple of minor exceptions, his byline would be D.L. Champion for the rest of his writing career.

Champion began hitting the pulps with regularity after 1937. The next year, in fact, would see the appearance of his first series character for Popular Publications, the aforementioned Inspector Allhoff. That began Champion's long and fruitful career as a creator of memorably off-kilter detectives. He wrote hundreds of one-off stories as well, mostly in a criminous vein. And over the subsequent 15 or so years, he was a success. While never making a movie sale—another brass ring for pulp writers—some of his work was adapted to radio, and a few of his longer pulp tales—including, amazingly enough, at least one Inspector Allhoff, "Shake Well Before Dying"—were offered as serials to newspapers around the world by King Features Syndicate.

According to John Locke, Champion also spent some time in the early '40s as a scripter for Funnies, Inc., a company that provided fully executed comic-book stories for various publications, including *Marvel Comics* No. 1.

Hanging in with the pulps until they expired in the early '50s, he turned to men's mags (*Hi-Life, Climax, Man's Day*) and true-crime publications (*Master Detective, Uncensored Detective, True Detective*), making an occasional sale to slick publications like *Coronet*. At this point, he was likely doing more nonfiction than fiction, and it's a good bet that he did more writing for the true-crime mags than has been discovered, since many of the stories in that genre were published without bylines. (For some reason, he reverted to the Jack D'Arcy nom de plume for a couple of '50s pieces, one for the pulp *Black Book Detective* and the other for *Master Detective*.)

During this time, in 1954, he divorced his first wife and married Eleanor Morehead, a writer for both the Associated Press and *P.M. Magazine* in New York before she returned home, probably with Champion in tow, for a job at Ohio's *Columbus Citizen-Journal* newspaper. (They had been a couple for some time before the marriage.) Her connection to her Columbus hometown explains why both she and Champion have their ashes interred in a mausoleum in that city, coincidentally once the site of the annual pulp-magazine celebration PulpFest.

In addition to his magazine work, Champion wrote at least two paperbacks, both of which deserve a bit of looking into. The first, *Run the Wild River*, came out from Lion Books in 1952; it was a novel about the then-hot topic of illegal Mexican immigration. The other, which was published by Lancer in 1967—the year before Champion's death—is *The Sexual Psychopath*, which deals with the case histories of seven notoriously crazy people through the ages. The cover calls it "AN IN-DEPTH STUDY BY A FAMOUS CRIME REPORTER OF THE SEXUALLY DERANGED CRIMINAL." Chances are good that at least some of the text was recycled by Champion from his true-crime magazine pieces.

The other is notable for its Mexican setting. That's the same country that provides the background for his Mariano Mercado tales. Which leads to the question: Why would a man who lived in New York for most of his life decide to write a novel and a pulp-detective series set in Mexico?

Of all people, famed novelist Saul Bellow has provided us with a possible answer.

VARIOUS SOURCES have Champion as a member of the British Army in World War I (unlikely, since he would've been in his mid-teens) as well as a member of the merchant marine. There doesn't appear to be any evidence to suggest he was either of those things, nor a World War II participant. He did register for the draft in February 1942 (as an alien), but his productivity as a writer through the war years suggest that he never served. So it's likely that he never was shipped out anywhere on the government's dime.

However, he did do some traveling. In the late '40s, for instance, he and fellow fictioneer Hal White traveled by plane to Puerto Rico, and a year later he and Eleanor took the SS *Neptune* to the Virgin Islands, where they spent a couple of months. There were a more trips to Puerto Rico as well.

But another foray out of New York, taken several years earlier, may have inspired—or at least help inspire—Mariano Mercado.

Information about this comes from a couple of sources. One is the British literary magazine *Granta*, whose 41st issue (published in 1992) contains a piece by James Atlas, the noted biographer, publisher, and editor. Titled "Starting Out in Chicago," it's about Bellow, and includes a section set in the summer of 1940, when the future Nobel Prize-winning author was living the Mexican town of Taxco. Located in a mountainous region, Taxco was, according to Atlas, "full of expatriates," including "eagle trainers Daniel and Jule Mannix; the publisher Joseph Hilton Smyth and his black girlfriend, the cabaret singer Hazel Scott; and D'arcy Lyndon Champion, an Australian who wrote pulp fiction for *Black Mask* and *Dime Detective*."

There's no indication how long Champion had been living in Taxco when Bellow and his wife arrived that summer, funded by a few hundred dollars from his late mother's insurance policy. In a series of letters to fellow novelist Philip Roth, which Roth excerpted and published in the April 17, 2005, *New Yorker*, Bellow wrote that once in the town, "I was intrigued with what I took to be the imaginative powers of the people I met... I wanted to see firsthand what the characters I was spending my time with were up to."

And, yes, one of those characters was D.L. Champion. Bellow wrote about drinking "far more than was good for me with American buddies in the zocalo (the town square)" and hanging out "with the hard-drinking professionals who wrote for *Black Mask* and other pulps. Mannix and his eagle were my antidotes to the low company of the pulp writers."

While Mannix was the inspiration for a character in Bellow's 1953 novel *The Adventures of Augie March*, it's uncertain whether or not Champion also provided grist for Bellow's fiction mill. There's also the matter of Bellow's plural nouns. Possibly, he was referring to both Champion and the above-mentioned Joseph Hilton Smyth, who'd been selling to the slicks since the late '20s and, as Joseph Hilton, had sold a quartet of stories to the less-prestigious *Stocking Parade* around 1939. And while he mentions the "low company" of pulp writers, that may have been at least partially in jest. Surely, they talked and even argued about their craft over endless rounds of drinks.

Although we don't know how long he lived there, Taxco certainly stayed with Champion. In this volume, for instance, one of the Mercado stories is partially set in that city, and another one mentions it. Logic indicates that Champion's time in the mountains (and bars) of Mexico went a long way toward providing him with the inspiration for his *detectivo particular.*

Saul Bellow went on to become one of America's great novelists. His Taxco drinking buddy went on to create Mercado, his final long-lived pulp character, in 1944, and to write scores of other fiction and nonfiction pieces for a wide variety of magazines. While you'd be hard-pressed to find two more disparate literary legacies, I find it somehow comforting to know that you can now find both these authors in the pages of their own books.

— John Wooley
Foyil, Oklahoma
30 September 2024

(Once again, my thanks to publisher Matt Moring, peerless researcher John Locke, and the FictionMags Index [philsp. com]. This time around, Peter McGarvey, John Gunnison, Steven Popper, and David Earle were also helpful, as was the Internet Broadway Database [IBDB].)

NO PLACE LIKE HOMICIDE

I SWEAR THAT MARIANO MERCADO SEEMED PLEASED BY THE NEWS OF GEORGE HARKWELL'S DEATH. IF A MAN HAD TO DIE IT WAS BETTER HE DID SO FROM A BULLET RATHER THAN FROM SUCCUMBING TO THE BACTERIAL HORDES. BUT DEATH BY VIOLENCE MEANS MURDER, AND MURDERERS HAVE TO BE CAUGHT. WHICH WAS WHY MERCADO AND I WERE IN NEW YORK, ON THE LAST LAP OF A SLAY-TRAIL WHICH STARTED ON THE GROUNDS OF THE AMERICAN EMBASSY IN MEXICO CITY AND ENDED IN A GUN SLINGING FREE-FOR-ALL IN A SIXTH AVENUE CHILI JOINT.

CHAPTER ONE
EMBASSY ENIGMA

I **CLIMBED** the stairs to Mariano Mercado's apartment in the Calle de Madellin, let myself in with my own latchkey. I found the little Mexican detective in his bedroom standing anxiously before a mirror, staring intently at his own coffee-colored features.

I said, *"Buenos días,"* and added: "What are you doing, admiring yourself?"

He did not turn around from his rapt contemplation of himself. He said: "Do you know that sunburn has been known to kill a man?"

"I've heard of a few isolated instances. But what do you care?"

He gestured with a thin and graceful hand to a copy of the newspaper *Universal* on the table. I glanced at it, saw that it was open to the English page. There was a two-column advertisement for a sunburn lotion.

I said: "I still don't get it."

"That advertisement," he said, turning around at last, "is addressed to the American tourists who are exposed to our brilliant sun only during the short period of their vacation. If they are in danger, what of me? I have faced this sun almost every day of my life."

I ran my fingers through my hair and sighed wearily. Every morning of his life Mariano Mercado became apprehensive that he was about to catch a new disease. Every afternoon he took drastic means to combat it. And mine was the ear into which was invariably poured the case history.

"Mercado," I said, "you can't possibly get sunburned."

"Why not?" he said piteously. "I am not a strong man. My constitution—"

"I am better acquainted with your constitution than you are. You can't get sunburned for the simple reason that you have lived under the Mexican sun all your life. You're immune. You can't get sunburned any more than a Hottentot."

We scrambled over the fence,
landed jarringly on the other side.
Crothers was nowhere in sight.

"Nevertheless," he said firmly, "I shall buy some of this lotion after we have eaten. We shall breakfast at Sanburn's."

Now, Sanburn's restaurant in Mexico City is as American as the Statue of Liberty. It caters to Americans and its cuisine is strictly United States.

"I thought you didn't like tourists," I said. "Nor American cooking. You'll find both at Sanburn's."

"True," said Mercado. "But our own restaurants of quality do not open until lunch time. The cheap places which are ready for custom now are dirty and unsanitary. I would rather expose myself to the execrable American food than to a horde of native bacteria."

"All right. Finish dressing."

He crossed the room and flung open his crammed closet. Then he proceeded to bedeck his thin wiry body. I gathered that as far as he was concerned, it was quite definitely Blue Monday. I do not mean that his hypochrondriac spirits had become depressed to the point of melancholy, nor that a Sunday evening orgy had brought on a racking hangover. The point I make is purely sartorial. It was his blue day.

His suit was the color of a robin's egg and it had been cut by a reckless, slashing hand. The lapels reached almost to his waistline and the shoulders were padded like an old quilt. The trousers had edges like swords and were as tight as a drum skin.

His shirt was the hue of the turquoise sky over Mexico City, his tie a trifle darker with a few restrained yellow stripes laced through it. His shoes were of two tones, each of them.

WE WENT downstairs into the street, walked through the sun to Sanborn's. As usual, it was crowded with tourists. In the babble of conversation, the only Spanish I heard was spoken by the waitresses.

As we sat down, I caught sight of a familiar bulky figure seated across the room, in an iris-piercing suit of yellow and green with a shirt of throbbing puce, that would make an angel sing off-key and his socks were a screaming saffron to match the stripes of his tie. He was in the company of a girl of about twenty-six. I said: "Look. There's your friend, *el coronel* Gomez."

Mercado turned his black eyes in the direction I had indicated. Gomez was an official of the police whose regard for Mercado was equaled only by Mercado's regard for him. Gomez was as honest as a roulette wheel in Juarez, a fact which Mercado didn't like at all. And Mercado was far more quick-witted than Gomez, a quality which the policeman could not abide.

Mercado turned back to the table, said: "No Mexican woman would trust Gomez. That is why he is compelled to find romance with a gringo tourist."

The girl looked from home, all right. She was a brunette with a pale, wistful face and a pair of big brown eyes that seemed to hold sadness within them.

"Romance?" I said. "At this hour in the morning? I doubt it."

Momentarily, we forgot Gomez and the girl and ordered fresh raspberries, eggs and coffee. We were half-way through our food when a high-pitched feminine voice sounded above the murmur of conversation in the room.

"Well, if he is, I'm going to see him!"

Mercado, his nose buried in his coffee cup, did not look up. I did. I saw Gomez apparently protesting, while the girl had half risen and was pointing a slim forefinger directly at the back of Mariano Mercado's spine.

"I think you're about to receive company," I told him.

Mercado removed his nose from his cup and bowed as Gomez and the girl approached the table. I stood up and pulled out a couple of chairs. Gomez beamed on us, a feat which I, at once, considered suspicious.

"This," he said in his heavy English, "is Miss Jane Harkwell."

We acknowledged the introduction. The girl said: "*Señor,* the waitress just mentioned to me that you are the best private detective in all Mexico."

Mercado admitted this charge with a modest bow.

"Then," she said, "I need your services. Have you seen the morning papers?"

Mercado sighed. "Dire tidings, indeed."

"Ah," said Jane Harkwell, "then you've heard about my uncle?"

"Your uncle?" said Mercado. "No, *señorita*, I refer to the typhus outbreak in the state of Oaxaca. I can give you some appalling statistics regarding typhus. This disease has slain more men than any war. Than all wars, as a matter of fact. I—"

"Mercado," I said hurriedly, "this lady seems in some distress."

He glared at me. He possessed more statistics than the Metropolitan Life Insurance Company and he handed them out freely, constantly and in stentorian tones.

"My uncle," said Jane Harkwell, "is dead."

Mercado evinced polite interest. "Of disease?"

She shook her head and as she answered her voice broke a little. "Of a bullet."

I swear Mercado seemed rather pleased by this news. If a man had to die it was far better he had done so by violence rather than from succumbing to the bacterial hordes.

He said: "Your uncle was murdered?"

"Of course, he was murdered," the girl said vehemently.

Gomez sighed heavily and entered the conversation for the first time.

"The *señorita* is naturally overwrought. Her uncle is a suicide. An unpleasant fact, but a fact nevertheless."

Mercado said coolly: "You have investigated?"

Gomez spread his palms upward. "It is out of my jurisdiction. However, it is obviously a suicide."

"That's idiotic," snapped the girl. "Why should my uncle kill himself?"

"I assume," said Mercado, "that the death did not take place in Mexico City?"

"Of course it did," said Jane Harkwell. "Right next door to the hotel where we are staying."

Mercado lifted his eyebrows and faced Gomez. "But, you, *señor*, said you had no jurisdiction. You have jurisdiction anywhere in Mexico City."

"Not everywhere," said Gomez softly. "This man killed himself on the property of the American Embassy. That is, under International Law, territory belonging to the United States of America."

Mercado ordered some more coffee. He said: "Perhaps you'd better tell me all about it."

Gomez cleared his throat. "It was this way, *amigo*. This *tourista* whose name is George Harkwell—"

Mercado held up a silencing brown hand. "It is the lady who is paying my fee," he said. "I will listen to her story."

GOMEZ LIT a cigarette unhappily. I gathered that he was not at all pleased to have Mercado mixed up in the matter.

"My uncle," began the girl, "is a lawyer. From New York. A client of his, Mr. Arthur Constance, had to come to Mexico on business. He needed a lawyer to come along so he brought my uncle. My uncle offered me the chance to take the trip with them. I speak a little Spanish and was supposed to make myself useful.

"Last night my uncle left our hotel to go to a drugstore. He was gone for quite a long time. At three o'clock this morning we phoned the police. They reported, after a while, that my uncle's body was lying before the Embassy. There was a bullet in his brain and a revolver in his hand."

"What hotel are you staying at?" asked Mercado.

"The Geneve. It is close to the Embassy."

"It was a suicide," said Gomez, twisting uncomfortably in his chair. "It is obvious. The gun is in his hand. According to the Embassy, his money and wallet were untouched. Doubtless, he was affected by some sentimentality which dictated that he die on American soil. Hence, he entered the Embassy property before he shot himself."

"A touching theory," said Mercado. "I can hardly imagine an American doing it. I cannot imagine a lawyer of any nationality at all doing it."

"He didn't do it," said Jane Harkwell vehemently.

"This Mr. Constance," said Mercado. "Did he believe your uncle had killed himself?"

"When he first heard the news he was most upset. He said my uncle had been murdered. But later he seemed to change his mind and to go over to the suicide theory."

"And you, you know of no reason why your uncle should have blown his brains out?"

"There wasn't any."

"*Pues,*" said Gomez, "who knows the innermost secrets of the human heart? Perhaps it was romantic trouble. An uncle would hardly take his niece into his confidence about such things."

Heaven knows I am not as shrewd as Mariano Mercado. However, it seemed to my dull wits that Gomez was desperately fighting for the suicide theory. I wondered why. Gomez was unscrupulous, but I was certain he had not stooped to the professional killing of tourists.

Mercado said: "Miss Harkwell, what was it that your uncle went out to buy at the drugstore?"

She shook her head. "I don't know. He didn't say."

"Did he speak Spanish?"

"None at all."

Gomez spread his palms again. His lips parted in his oiliest smile. *"Amigos,"* he said, "why all this pointless questioning? The man is dead. We Mexicans murder for only two reasons, robbery or jealousy. Señor Harkwell was not robbed. He had not been in the city long enough to have established a liaison which would cause an angry husband to shoot him."

Mercado said to me: "Latham, go to the telephone. Call the Geneve Hotel. If Harkwell spoke no Spanish, he must have asked the desk clerk where a drugstore was situated. Perhaps he even asked how to order what he wanted in our language. Find out."

I went off to the telephone booth. Personally, I had no theory as to the death of Harkwell. However, I did know that the Mexican police didn't like dead Americans, nor did the Embassy. Tourists' corpses invariably cluttered up international relations.

I made my phone call, chatted to the desk clerk for a full ten minutes and returned with the information Mercado desired.

"You were right," I told him. "Harkwell asked the clerk both questions."

"Bueno. And what did he want at the drugstore?"

"Bicarbonate of soda."

Mercado grinned at Gomez. *"Coronel,"* he said, "the man was murdered."

"That theory is idiotic," said Gomez. "Do you mean to tell me that any Mexican would have the nerve to murder a man on the grounds of the American Embassy?"

Mercado shook his head. "No. The man was not murdered there at all. Moreover, you cannot tell me that a man buys bicarbonate of soda, then kills himself. A bullet will cure his heartburn much more quickly than bicarbon-ate. The drug was unnecessary to a potential suicide."

"But the body. It was on the Embassy grounds. You can't get away from that, my friend. You can't—"

"Wait," said Mercado, and his black eyes twinkled. When he spoke again it was in Spanish. "Let me tell you a story. It is a gringo story. From Brooklyn. Listen."

I GAVE him my full attention. Mercado was not a friv-olous character. If he digressed before a potential client to relate an anecdote from Brooklyn, quite obviously it had a point.

"There was a policeman," began Mercado, still speaking in his native tongue, "a Brooklyn policeman who, unlike yourself, *mi coronel,* was a stupid illiterate officer. There came a day when he found a dead horse lying in the street. To be precise, on Kosciusko Street.

"The officer rolled up his sleeves, bent over and proceeded to drag the horse along the pavement. A bystander approached and asked the policeman what he was doing.

" 'I've found a dead horse,' replied the policeman, 'and I have to make a report of the matter.'

" 'So,' said the bystander, 'and where are you taking it?'

" 'I'm dragging it down to Hoyt Street.'

" 'Why?'

" 'Because,' said the policeman, 'I just can't spell Kosciusko.' "

There was a long blank silence. I realized that Jane Hark-well's limited knowledge of Spanish precluded her follow-ing Mercado's story. As for myself, I understood the words, all right, but I was damned if I understood the point. I glanced at Gomez to see his reaction.

He was glaring at Mercado. His swarthy cheeks were hot and dark. He twirled his mustache in the manner of a man who is angry.

Mercado smiled faintly, said: "You do not like my anecdote, *coronel?*" He sighed and shook his head. "It is very funny in English."

Gomez uttered an obscene Spanish oath, pushed his chair back across the elaborately tiled floor and stood up. He repeated the oath, turned on his heel and strode from the restaurant.

Jane Harkwell asked: "What has happened?"

"I hate to admit this," said Mariano Mercado, "but I am forced to concede that laziness and a desire to avoid work and responsibility are pronounced traits of our nation."

I emptied my coffee cup. Nettled, I said: "Would you stop being so cryptic? Would you mind explaining your last philosophical observation? Also your Brooklyn story. Also tell me what all this has to do with the death of Miss Harkwell's uncle."

"He was murdered," said Mercado. "And *not* on the grounds of the American Embassy. Doubtless he was killed on the Calle Niza."

"Then how did the corpse get to the Embassy?"

"It was dragged there."

"By whom?"

"One of Gomez' men."

Jane Harkwell blinked. "You mean the police put him there?"

Mercado nodded. "It has happened before. It is remarkable, but of every ten Americans who die violently in Mexico City, six of them are discovered on the property of the United States Embassy."

I thought back to his story of Kosciusko Street and all of a sudden a light hit me.

"I see what you mean," I said. "The tourist trade is one of Mexico's principal industries. It must not be discouraged. Moreover, dead Americans are international situations. The government will not like it. The police will be compelled to dig up the criminal. In order to save all this trouble, the bodies of dead Americans are, on occasion, dragged onto Embassy property. It is then strictly an affair of the United States."

"*Es verdad,*" said Mariano Mercado. "*El coronel* Gomez is not an energetic man."

"Nor an honest one," flared Jane Harkwell. "He knows very well it was no suicide. But it's easier for him to call it that."

Mercado nodded his head in slow agreement. "*Sí*, I fear, *señorita*, that he is not honest either."

"Then," said Jane Harkwell, "consider yourself retained. I will pay you anything within reason, and you are to find the killer."

"For money," murmured Mercado, "I will try anything."

"Except," I put in, "undistilled water."

Mercado shuddered and looked at me reproachfully. He said: "Let us go to your hotel and call on Mr. Constance."

CHAPTER TWO
THE ROAD TO UTOPIA

I CALLED the waitress and paid the check. A few minutes later the three of us were in a taxicab bound for the luxurious Hotel Geneve.

We disembarked, strode through the tiled lobby and ascended to the third floor. Jane Harkwell knocked on a door and in response to a bass, "Come in," we entered.

Constance was a little man. He was almost bald, the few remaining gray wisps of hair plastered down on his shining pate. His mustache, however, was luxuriant. His spinal column was concave and it struck me that he was probably much younger than he looked. I guessed he was just the wrong side of fifty.

The girl introduced us. As she announced Mercado's profession, Constance shot her a sharp glance of annoyance. Then he waved us to chairs. He spoke in a rather high-pitched voice.

"Miss Harkwell," he said, "is naturally upset. For that we cannot blame her. But I assure you that this is no case for a detective. Harkwell killed himself. I am certain of that."

Mercado lifted his eyebrows. "According to Miss Harkwell, you didn't think so when first you heard of his death."

"The man who called me stated flatly that he had been killed. Of course, the news upset me and I hadn't time to think. Later when I heard the police theory, I recalled what I knew of Harkwell's private affairs and I was in accord with the official theory."

"Do you mean," said Mercado, "that you know why he killed himself?"

Constance nodded. "Well, yes," he said, glancing uncomfortably at the girl. "I hadn't wanted to tell you this, Jane. But since you're convinced that George was murdered, I am more or less forced to tell you the truth."

Jane Harkwell stared at him. There was skepticism and unfriendliness in her eyes.

"There was a woman back home who was plaguing him. I'm afraid she had letters and various other things which would have caused George a lot of trouble. He got a letter from her last night, a letter which made impossible demands. Had he refused there would have been a nasty scandal. He would have been disbarred and ruined."

Jane Harkwell said shortly: "I don't believe it."

Mercado was frowning and thoughtful. As far as I could see he wasn't getting anywhere. Even if Constance were lying there was nothing Mercado could do about it. And if there had been any clues lying about at the time when Gomez' copper found the corpse, they certainly were cold by now.

A knock came at the door of the suite. Constance said: "Come in."

A man of medium height entered the room. For a moment, I was uncertain as to whether he was Mexican or American. His skin was brown but whether from sunburn or heritage it was difficult to say. When he spoke it was in English but with what seemed to me the faintest trace of a Spanish accent. Yet when he said, *"Buenos dias,"* to Mercado, I thought I heard an American taint in his Spanish. But there was no doubt of the fact that he spoke in the deepest bass since Chaliapin.

Constance said: "This is Señor Huerta."

Señor Huerta beamed on us all. Constance said to Jane Harkwell: "Mr. Huerta is returning to the States with us."

Her thin eyebrows arched. "Why?"

"This is the man we were looking for. Your uncle found him for me."

Jane Harkwell seemed puzzled but suspicious. She said to Huerta: "You knew Harry Crothers?"

Huerta shook his head and clucked like an old hen. "Indeed," he said. "My best friend. I was with him when he died."

"He's dead?"

"*En verdad.* He has been dead for some three years."

Jane Harkwell stood up. She walked over to the window and looked out into the tree-lined street. She turned her head abruptly.

"Señor Mercado," she said, "may I see you at your office this afternoon?"

"*Porqué no?*" said Mercado. "Always provided it does not disturb my siesta hour."

"Four o'clock."

"Four o'clock," said Mercado, leaving his chair and walking to the door.

I got up and followed him. At the door he bowed gravely to everyone and went out into the corridor. I still followed.

In the lobby, Mercado made his way through a crowd of chattering tourists to the desk clerk. He slid a five-peso note across the marble counter.

"Last night," he said, "you will remember Señor Constance getting word that his friend was dead?"

The clerk nodded. "Yes. The Embassy sent a man over here after they had identified the body from some mail found in his pocket."

"And did the *señor* have any other visitors last night?"

"None, *señor.*"

"But he had a telephone call?"

"He did, *señor.*"

"And that would have been about an hour after the man from the Embassy was here?"

"That is correct, *señor.*"

"*Gracias,*" said Mercado. "And that was his only call all night?"

The clerk nodded and after thanking him we went out into the street to look for a taxi.

I LEANED back in the seat and thought it all over. I didn't talk about it until we were back in the Calle de Madellin apartment.

"Of course," I said, "I see what you were driving at with the desk clerk. You figured that if Constance said it was murder the first time something must have happened to make him change his mind. Something external. Something like a visitor or a phone call."

Mercado nodded abstractedly. He was engaged in shaking out three vitamin pills into his palm. He meticulously placed them on the healthiest looking tongue I had seen in years and washed them down with a glass of water.

"Correct," said Mercado. "I believe that Señor Constance is lying—with all the assurance of a man who cannot be questioned."

"What are you going to do? I gathered from Constance's words that he will return home shortly. You haven't much time."

"I have no time at all," said Mercado equably.

"What do you mean by that?"

"We wash our hands of it."

"And lose the fee?"

"What else? I can't demand information of the Embassy. Gomez would give me none even if he had it. Constance, who is lying, can call the police if I bother him. What am I to do? Pick a killer out of thin air? Now, let us go to lunch."

"Isn't it early for lunch?"

"The sooner we eat it the sooner we may repair to our siesta and rest the tissues of our body."

Glumly, I went along with him. It wasn't every day we got a case with a cash fee, but I was forced to agree with him. After all, he was no crystal-gazer.

I went back to Mercado's place after my siesta. I found him busily engaged in routing whatever germs had settled upon him while he slept. He gargled vigorously with two beautifully colored mouthwashes, performed his ablutions with a disinfected soap which smelled far worse than most unsanitary odors, then swallowed two teaspoonsful of two different medicines as a general tonic.

No sooner had he finished than the door bell rang and I admitted Jane Harkwell. She nodded to me and strode purposefully to Mercado's desk.

"Señor Mercado," she said, "I want you to come to New York."

Mercado blinked. He had never been in New York. As a matter of fact he hadn't been in the United States since he was a child. His ideas about the country were somewhat confused. He pictured everything north of the Border as a germ-free, brightly scrubbed, shining land.

"I shall pay all your expenses," said Jane Harkwell, "and also five thousand pesos for your time."

"It is true," asked Mercado tremulously, like a child asking to be reassured regarding Santa Claus, "that in New York the water is so pure it may be drunk from the bathroom faucet?"

"It is true," said Jane Harkwell.

"I shall go," said Mercado. Then he added rather querulously: "Why?"

Jane Harkwell sighed and sat down on one of Mariano Mercado's thoroughly antiseptic chairs.

"Because you're the only person with enough sense to know that my uncle was murdered. And because I have a strong premonition that something's wrong and I have enough money to indulge myself."

"But what do you want me to do?"

She shrugged her slim shoulders. "I'm not even sure of that. But I'm positive something odd is going on. I want you to help me find out what it is. Perhaps the answer to my uncle's death is in New York. It's certainly not here."

Mercado's face was suddenly grave. He leaned forward over his desk, said: "Do you believe that Arthur Constance killed your uncle?"

She hesitated for a long moment, then said frankly: "I never liked Constance. I think he's lying now about my uncle having had some trouble with a woman. I believe he'd be capable of murder, provided there was enough money in it. But I don't see *how* he could have killed my uncle that night. I was with him all the time my uncle was out of the hotel, save for about ten minutes when I went to my own room to get a handkerchief."

Mercado nodded. "Constance said that this man Huerta was the fellow your uncle had found for him. What did he mean by that?"

"I'll tell you. It's one of the reasons I want you to come back home with me. My mother is dead. Her best friend was an elderly widow who became totally blind as the result of an accident a few years ago. Her name is Alicia Crothers and she is extremely wealthy. Arthur Constance is going to marry her."

"And you don't approve of the match?" said Mercado.

"I do not. But Mrs. Crothers is lonely and troubled. She won't listen to me. However, she was very much in love with her husband who disappeared some twenty years ago. She flatly refused to marry Constance until it was definitely proved that her husband was dead. My uncle got a tip that he had died here in Mexico. That's why we came—to check on it."

Mercado nodded. "So now it's checked—with this Huerta—and Constance will wed the wealthy widow. How wealthy is she?"

"Millions," said Jane Harkwell. "That's why I think something funny is going on."

Some time later, after Miss Harkwell had left, Mercado turned to me, his copper face beaming. "Latham," he said, "this is a great moment. We travel north to the United States, where there are no germs, no slums, no disease, a veritable sanitary Utopia. For once my poor mind will be free from worry."

I let him dwell in his fool's Paradise. I didn't tell him about the horrible tenements on New York's lower East Side. I didn't tell him of the cockroach-ridden slum apartments. I didn't tell him of the appalling infant mortality rate of this, my native land.

We left two days later. Exercising great restraint, or possibly because he fondly believed he was traveling to a realm where there were no bacteria, Mercado brought along a mere half dozen medicine bottles and a scant three boxes of pills.

THE TRAIN pulled out of Buena Vista Station at twenty minutes past eight in the evening. Mercado and I occupied a Pullman section. Opposite us, Jane Harkwell had a lower. Arthur Constance and Huerta had a compartment in the car ahead of us.

Constance had spotted us boarding the train. He had cocked an inquiring eyebrow but asked no questions. Jane Harkwell read a magazine grimly for a while and was in her berth before the train had passed through Calera.

I wondered if she had told Constance that we had been retained or whether he merely thought it coincidental that we were on the same train. If that were his idea, I figured it would be dispelled when he saw us still with him at the Border.

We went through Monterrey at six o'clock the following evening and were due at Laredo, in Texas, at midnight. Now the last stop before the American Border is the little town of Camaron. The train pulled up at the ramshackle station at exactly a quarter to eleven.

Mercado was sitting by the window, staring into the moonlit night with his dark and brooding eyes. Suddenly he became erect in his chair. He nudged me and pointed.

Huerta had stepped on to the station platform from the train, and at that moment the train started up again. Huerta made no attempt to reboard the car. He walked swiftly through the station to the dirt road beyond it.

Mercado shrugged. "I thought Constance was taking him along to testify to the death of Crothers."

"So did I. Perhaps he merely got a written attestation from him instead."

"Then why bring him all the way north to Camaron?"

I didn't know the answer to that, nor did I consider it particularly important. Mercado apparently did. His brow was wrinkled and there was a thoughtful expression in his dark eyes when we went through the customs at the Border.

Customs and immigration inspection held us up for the usual three hours and it was quite late when we were able to turn in. I was sleepy and irritable when Mercado and I entered the diner at San Antonio for breakfast.

We had barely attacked our eggs when two men entered and sat at the table opposite us. One of them was Constance, who gave us a nod that was barely civil, the other was Huerta in an equally unsociable mood.

I gaped at them. I turned back to Mercado and said: "But he got off at Camaron. How did he get back on the train?"

Mercado looked at me sleepily. "I am not surprised," he announced. "I thought about it a great deal last night. I rather expected that we had not seen the last of Señor Huerta."

I asked him a half a dozen more questions, but despite my curiosity he wasn't talking. Then Jane Harkwell came in and sat down with us and the conversation took other turns.

The remainder of the trip was uneventful. Mercado was oddly silent. He stared out of the train window and seemed lost in thought. I guessed he was meditating on the strange actions of Señor Huerta, and left him alone while I buried my nose in a book.

When we arrived at New York, Constance and Huerta bade us curt farewells and hurried out of the station. Jane Harkwell accompanied us to a phone booth from which we tried to round up a couple of rooms in a hotel.

I did the phoning while Mercado beamed around the station. The floor was well swept which delighted him. The crowds that passed were not afflicted with *pinta* or any other obvious disease. It struck me that for once in his life he had lost his awful fear of contagion.

After some difficulty, we managed to obtain a couple of rooms in a small hotel within three blocks of Mrs. Crothers' apartment. I slept soundly and awakened refreshed and energetic after nine hours' rest.

I showered and dressed, then went out into the hall and knocked at the door of Mercado's room. A shaky, unhappy voice said: "Come in."

I WENT in to find Mercado sitting huddled in a huge armchair. His ear was glued to the radio and there was a fearful expression on his face.

"Where is a *farmacia?*" he asked.

"This town is lousy with *farmacias*," I said.

"What do you want now?"

He pointed a trembling finger at the radio. "Everything," he said. "*Dios*, I have nothing. I did not realize. I did not know."

"Did not know what?"

"The risks one runs. I have been listening to the radio. I have learned some terrible things."

"For instance?"

"About my health. There are so many things I must take to guard against disease. I never dreamed—"

I laughed. I could easily see that Mercado, after getting a load of the radio commercials, was more worried about germs than ever before.

"I need laxatives," he said. "Several of them. Each contains an ingredient peculiar to that specific laxative alone. I will need them all. And several toothpastes to keep my mouth free of bacteria. And many breakfast foods for iron, roughage and protein. *Dios*, Latham, I simply can't swallow everything I am supposed to take."

He stared at me gloomily. "I never should have come. Ignorance is bliss. I just didn't know the danger. I thought that in the United States I would be free from these worries. I thought—"

"Forget it," I said. "Our advertising agencies invented hypochondria. How about some breakfast?"

Moodily, he got out of the chair. I could see that he was shaken. The oily voice of some announcer who had predicted dire happenings to those who didn't use his product still echoed in Mercado's soul.

He put on his hat, wrapped himself up against the outside air and we went downstairs.

Directly opposite us was a chili joint. Mercado stared at it. A bright neon sign twinkled outside. Within, its counter was of gleaming white tile. The floor was spotless. The chairs were of glittering chrome and red leather.

Mercado smiled and some of his gloom vanished.

"Look," he said, "here we can eat chili for breakfast. In a place that is clean, free of germs. Not like the places in Mexico City where one dares not tread. Come on."

Personally, I didn't want chili for breakfast, but if it could make Mercado forget the constant unseen death which filtered through the air it was all right with me.

We went in and sat a counter. Mercado ate two bowls of chili and so impressed was he with American standards of sanitation that he neglected to perform his customary ritual of wiping off each dish and piece of cutlery with a silk handkerchief.

He ate with relish. Temporarily, he actually forgot his fear of germs. He drained his cup, turned to me and said: "Ah, poor Mexico. Here, in a cheap restaurant, we have the ultimate in cleanliness and sanitation. In my country, for those essentials one must patronize the most expensive places."

There were several things I could have told him about sanitation in New York. For both our sakes, I kept my mouth shut.

We returned to the hotel to find Jane Harkwell waiting in the lobby. She greeted us in a worried voice.

"Perhaps I'm a fool," she said. "Mr. Constance is most angry at me for bringing you up here. He says I'm a silly, hysterical woman. And I admit I sound that way when the only reason I can give him for bringing you up here is that I felt a premonition."

Personally, I had thought the same thing since the very beginning. It didn't make sense to come to New York to find the killer of a man who had been slain in Mexico. However, with me a free ride was a free ride and I hadn't been home for three years.

But Mariano Mercado shook his head. "I do not consider you a silly woman," he said gravely. "As a matter of fact I am beginning to have a premonition myself."

Jane Harkwell seized on this eagerly. "You mean you think something is wrong?"

"Emphatically," said Mercado. "Suppose you introduce us to your friend, Mrs. Crothers."

I said: "Are you working on a murder committed in Mexico or on the protection of Mrs. Crothers?"

He turned to me, mild surprise on his face. He said: "You don't think they're unconnected, do you?"

ALICIA CROTHERS was a little woman. She sat in a huge armchair, looking like a China doll. Her sightless eyes stared straight ahead in a dim room with drawn shades. She was dressed in a black bombazine affair which covered her entire body like a voluminous shroud.

She appeared to be well over fifty years of age. A maid, older than her mistress, led us into the vast rectangular living room. Jane Harkwell went forward to greet her. Then she introduced Mercado and myself as two old friends whom she had met in Mexico.

Alicia Crothers gave us her blue-veined hand. She said in a remarkably clear voice: "Jane, you must bring your friends to the wedding."

There was a moment's silence. Jane Harkwell said: "Then you really intend to marry him?"

The old woman nodded. "Why not? He seems to be a gentleman. And I'm lonely. I need someone to look after the estate. I have only delayed this long because I was never certain of Harry's fate. I never loved anyone but him. I must be sure he is dead before I marry again."

The girl said: "I take it you've spoken to Mr. Constance since he got back?"

"On the telephone. He has this Mr. Huerta with him. Mr. Huerta was with Harry when he died." She sighed heavily. "It is a relief to have some word after all these years even if it is only of his death."

Mercado said softly: "How many years, madam?"

"Twenty-eight. Harry just disappeared. Vanished. I never knew why. I locked up his room two weeks after he had gone. It has never been unlocked since. For years I wondered why he had left. I never found out. Now, even my curiosity is leaving me."

She sighed again. "Mr. Constance has been kind to me. As my husband, he will know how to distribute my estate so it brings more good to the world than it has to an unhappy old woman."

Jane Harkwell looked unhappy. She glanced over toward Mercado who shook his head, tacitly counselling the avoidance of what the young woman was about to say.

After about twenty minutes we took our leave. In the street, I said: "Well, now what? What is this all about, if anything?"

Mercado said: "Latham, I need a detective."

"Hell, you *are* a detective!"

"That won't do. I have not authority and thus far no law of this state has been broken. I want a private detective. Where can we find one?"

I shrugged my shoulders. My acquaintance with private detectives prior to meeting Mariano Mercado had been limited to fiction.

"We can try the classified directory," I said.

"Good. Let's."

From the pages of that invaluable book we selected a gentleman named Joseph Mendoza. It was a haphazard selection dictated solely because of Mr. Mendoza's obvious Spanish ancestry.

We took a taxi down town to the forties where Mendoza's office was situated between Sixth and Seventh Avenues.

CHAPTER THREE
UNHOLY MATRIMONY

MENDOZA WAS an elderly man, fat and possessed of a pair of darkly suspicious eyes. His office was shabby enough to cause Mercado to perch gingerly on the edge of the chair he sat in. I knew as soon as he got back to the hotel he would embark on a purification rite to get rid of whatever germs hung out in Mendoza's office.

This time I couldn't blame him too much. The furniture was broken and dirty. The desk was battered and obviously had been secondhand a decade before. The carpet was scuffed and worn. Even I could well believe that Mr. Mendoza's office was a breeding place for bacteria.

Before Mercado could state his business, Mendoza took a few minutes to tell us how good he was.

"Yes, sir," he said affably, "I was with the New York Police Department for twenty-five years. The finest bunch of coppers in the world. I have my pension and could quit entirely. But there's so much bloodhound in me I just have to keep at it. Now, sir, is it a divorce?"

I suspected that most of Mendoza's business came from divorces, and that if there wasn't any evidence Mr. Mendoza would be glad to manufacture some for you.

Mercado shook his head. "No, not a divorce but something just as simple. Staying with a Mr. Arthur Constance at 1168 East 119th Street is a man named Huerta. I want you to check on him for me."

Mendoza wrote down the name and address. "Check in what way?"

"See if he has any record. It should be simple enough for you to obtain a set of his fingerprints. I'd like them checked at Police Headquarters. I suppose you can manage that?"

"Indeed," said Mendoza. "The police will do anything for me. Is that all?"

"That's all at this time," said Mercado. "What do you charge?"

"Twenty bucks a day and expenses."

Mercado shook his head. This was added proof that all Americans were millionaires. He considered himself lucky if he got half that much. Reluctantly, he handed over a twenty-dollar bill.

"Come back about this time tomorrow," said Mendoza, "and I'll let you know what I've got. And bring another twenty bucks in case I can't do it all today."

We went out into the street. I didn't have a very high opinion of Mendoza and I said so. Mercado shrugged. "It doesn't make much difference. It takes little intelligence to do what I have asked."

I glanced at him curiously. "What's on your mind? Do you think Huerta's a crook or something?"

"Obviously," said Mercado. "Now, let us go back to the immaculate place where they sell the chili and have some lunch."

I sighed and went along. Apparently, I was going to be forced to eat chili all during our stay. It was a dish I could happily do without and which I rarely ate in Mexico.

We did the town that night. I didn't particularly relish sitting in crowded nightclubs but I figured I was only letting myself in for a lot of trouble if I permitted Mercado to sit home and listen to the messages of impending doom on the radio.

We breakfasted once more in the chili joint and I was forced to listen to another encomium of Mercado's on the polished appearance of the joint. When we got back to the hotel we had a visitor. It was Constance.

He came into the room, rubbing his hands and exuding good will.

"Gentlemen," he said, "I suppose I owe you an apology."

I didn't know why and I said so.

"It was really my job to override Miss Harkwell's whim. She's dragged you up here for no good purpose that I can see on a wild goose chase. It was foolish of me to permit it. I am here to make amends."

Mercado swallowed one of his after-breakfast pills. I didn't know exactly what it was supposed to cure. After the previous day's session at the radio he had promptly spent a fortune in the local drugstore, despite my loud protests.

"Yes," said Constance, "I suppose that silly girl has already defrayed your expenses up here and paid you some sort of a fee. Well, I am prepared to pay your way back and give you a check for five hundred dollars for your trouble. Naturally, you will keep whatever she has given you, also."

It sounded like a beautiful deal to me. We'd had a free trip and we'd get back to Mexico with enough cash in our pockets to loaf around for a while.

Moreover, as far as I could see, we were doing no good here. Whether Crothers' widow married Constance or not made no difference at all to me. And despite Mercado's sinister hinting I didn't see that any terrible crime was about to be perpetrated.

"I am sorry," said Mariano Mercado. "I work only for one client at a time. I am committed to Miss Harkwell."

"Committed to what?" said Constance loudly. His face flushed with color. "To what? Why are you here? Don't tell me you expect to find out anything about her uncle's death here in New York?"

Mercado nodded. "That is precisely what I *do* expect."

Constance stared at him, exasperated, for several seconds, then turned on his heel and left the room. I made a futile gesture and said: "Why did you turn him down? Why are you always tossing money away?"

He didn't answer. He put on his porkpie hat and said: "Let us go down and see if Mendoza has found out anything."

I sighed and went downstairs with him. We took a taxi downtown.

HALF AN hour later we were inside Mr. Mendoza's shabby office. So was Mr. Mendoza. Mr. Mendoza was not so garrulous this morning—and there was an excellent reason for this metamorphosis.

Mendoza lay on the floor of his office, half his body underneath his ancient desk. There was an ugly gash in his throat. Blood soaked into the dusty, thirsty carpet. It needed no medical examiner to know that Mendoza was dead, nor, for that matter, how he had died.

Mercado stared down at the corpse. He said in a loud voice: *"Dios,* I have killed him." He clapped his palm against his forehead and said it again, still louder.

"Don't be an idiot," I snapped. "And let's get out of here. This isn't Mexico City. We don't know a copper in town and we haven't a single connection. Let someone else find the body and for heaven's sake stop telling the world at the top of your voice that you killed him."

Mercado blinked at me. For one of the few times in his life he decided without argument that I was entirely right. He backed across the room to the door, opened it and went out of the office: I was so close behind him that I trod on his small and highly polished shoes.

In the taxi, I said breathlessly: "Let's call Constance."

"Why?"

"This, I think, is an excellent time to tell him that we've reconsidered, that we'll accept his proposition. We can be on a plane tonight. There isn't anyone who can connect us with Mendoza's death."

"There's someone I can connect with it," said Mercado. "And I'm going to stay here until I do."

"Where are we going now?"

"To Mrs. Crothers."

"Why?"

"There's one question I want to ask her before I go to the police."

I knew better than to argue with him although I was still certain that our best course was to snap up a fast check from Constance and grab the first plane south.

Mrs. Crothers' maid admitted us. She invited us to seat ourselves in the foyer since her mistress was engaged at the moment. We sat down on a pair of upholstered chairs.

Mercado looked uneasy. I attributed this to the fact that he was terrified of all cushioned chairs. Microscopic life bred in them.

From the living room we could hear the sound of voices. One definitely was that of Mrs. Crothers, one equally definitely was that of Constance. Then there was a third voice, that of a man, which I had never heard before.

The conversation resolved itself into a low inarticulate rumble as it came through the closed door. None of the words was intelligible.

Some twenty minutes later, the living room door opened. The maid appeared and ushered Constance and Huerta to the front door. I waited for someone else to appear but there was no one else in the room.

Constance bowed coldly, paused as if he were about to speak to us, then at a signal from Huerta kept going on out of the apartment. Huerta, a grim expression on his face, followed.

The maid announced us, then told us to go in. I followed Mercado into the room, still puzzled.

The third voice I had heard most certainly was not Huerta's. I'm no expert on the human voice, but Huerta's bass was so low-pitched, so distinctive that I would have recognized it anywhere.

"Madam," said Mercado, "since we know each other so slightly you will think I have come here with a strange request."

The old woman looked at him blankly. "What is it?"

"It is a request that you trust me. It is even more important to you than it is to me."

There was a long silence in the room. Mrs. Crothers sighed. "Jane said I was to trust you. And I trust Jane—implicitly. What is it?"

"That room," said Mercado, "that room of your husband's which has been locked all these years. Has no one ever been in it at all?"

"No one."

"Perhaps there is a safe in the room?"

"There is. A wall safe."

"And no one has opened that safe either? No one since your husband?"

She shook her head. "No one. I don't even know the combination myself. But why do you ask these things?"

Now Mercado hesitated. He said softly: "Perhaps I can give your husband back to you."

She started violently in her chair. "But he's dead," she said. "He's dead."

"I doubt it," said Mercado. He added in a voice which she could not hear: "Although it might be better so."

He stood up, said: "We shall return in a few hours with Miss Harkwell."

WE WENT out of the apartment and into a corner saloon where Mercado asked for *habanero.* To the bartender his request was as unintelligible as Choctaw. We both settled for Scotch and soda.

Mercado gulped his drink. He turned his brown face to me and it was grave and worried. His eyes were shadowed and he wore a deep frown.

This was an extremely odd circumstance. Excluding his phobia on bacterial life, Mercado was not a man given to brooding. I said: "What's the matter?"

He made a gesture of futility with his palms spread upward, then he said: "I am a duck out of water. In a foreign land. Latham, I must get a policeman. A trustworthy policeman, one who has been on the Force a long time."

I thought this over, said: "I can do the next best thing for you. I know a police reporter who's been on the Headquarters beat for twenty years. He'll know someone. And if you can promise him a story we should have him in the palms of our hands."

"Bueno," he said. "Call him."

I went into a phone booth and called Larry Gale. After exchanging the usual greetings people exchange when they haven't heard from one another for four or five years I came to the point.

"Sure," he said, "I got a guy—Phelan. He's a sergeant. We do each other favors. And he's been on the Force since Peter Stuyvesant was Mayor. I'll come along if you think there's a story."

I hung up and reported to Mercado. "Good," he said. "Call him back and find out where I can meet this Phelan. It must be right away. While I'm down seeing him you call the Harkwell girl. Then the two of you go back to the Crothers place and wait for me."

I went back to the phone booth and made the necessary arrangements. Then I returned to Mercado's side.

"At Police Headquarters. Centre Street," I told him. "They'll be waiting for you. Now what am I supposed to do in the Crothers place?"

"Wait for me. And see that nothing happens."

"Nothing happens? Nothing like what?"

"Murder," he said quietly, "or marriage."

He emptied his glass and dashed out into the street to hail a taxi. I sighed, phoned Jane Harkwell and asked her to meet me at the Crothers apartment.

I met the Harkwell girl in the hall of the apartment house, which was lucky. I doubt that I would have gained admittance alone. Constance and Huerta were already there. The old lady was dressed fit to kill. Her gnarled hands glittered with diamonds. She wore a silk dress, heaven only knows how old, and her head was wrapped in some lace gadget.

The men looked at us unpleasantly as we entered, but the old woman fluttered with happiness. She said to Jane: "I'm so glad you're here, dear. We've decided to wait no longer. A justice of the peace is on the way now."

Jane glanced at Constance. He returned her gaze coolly.

"There's no point in waiting. Alicia needs someone to straighten out her mixed financial affairs immediately. Naturally, it will be a simpler matter if I am her husband."

I cleared my throat, said: "In case the justice of the peace arrives before Mercado, I trust, Mrs. Crothers, you will wait for my friend."

She smiled. "Of course, we want him to witness the ceremony."

"Why?" snapped Constance. "What's he got to do with it? I don't know why Jane brought him here anyway. Why should we wait?"

The argument was still going on when the doorbell rang. To my relief it was Mariano Mercado. With him was a bulky man with an Irish face, bushy eyebrows and the air of a copper. This, then, was Phelan.

Jane Harkwell said: "We are waiting for an official to arrive and marry these two people."

Mercado smiled faintly and sat down. "I think," he said, "it might be advisable to postpone the ceremony for a while, Mrs. Crothers."

Constance stood up. His face was purple. "Why do all you people insist on butting into affairs which don't concern you?" he cried. "We want to get married. We're well over twenty-one and we know our minds. Adults may do as they please in this country."

"Not always," said Mercado softly.

"What do you mean by that?"

"Well," said Mercado, "there are several things one is not permitted to do—among them being arson, assault, and cutting the throat of a private detective in his own office, for instance."

Constance gasped. Huerta cleared his throat and looked at Mercado through slitted eyelids. Mrs. Crothers said: "What on earth is the matter? Why, pray, should I postpone my wedding?"

"Because," said Mercado, "while it is true that your husband is legally dead, Mrs. Crothers, it is also true that he is actually alive."

THERE WAS a moment of taut silence in the room. "Do you mean that Mr. Huerta has been lying to me?" the old woman asked.

"Only partially," said Mercado. "It is true, indeed, that he was your husband's best friend. It is most dubious that your husband died in his arms."

There was another silence. All of us looked at Mercado. Phelan leaned up against the wall, idly picking his teeth. Despite his casual air, his eyes never left Mercado's face.

Alicia Crothers leaned forward in her chair. "You mean my husband is alive?"

"That is what I mean," said Mariano Mercado. "But I do not think he will be alive long."

"You mean he's ill?"

"No," said Mercado, "I mean he is a killer. He was a killer twenty-eight years ago. That's why he ran away. He was a crook and a murderer. But the police didn't know him by the name of Crothers. To them he was Amos Widders. So he fled the country and you never heard of him again."

"You're a meddling liar," said Constance in a tone which convinced me that he thought Mercado anything but a liar. "Can you prove any of these things?"

"All of them," said Mercado.

Phelan sighed. He shifted the toothpick from one side of his mouth to the other and said: "How about getting started, bud?"

Mercado glanced at him and showed almost all of his excellent teeth. "Well," he said, "so Widders disappeared. And it never became necessary to look for him until Mr. Constance met Mrs. Crothers and heard of her vast wealth. He promptly asked her to become his wife and was accepted conditionally."

"The condition being," I put in, "that she be assured of her missing husband's demise."

"Precisely," said Mercado.

I looked over at Constance, expecting to see him verging on apoplexy. He wasn't. His face was deathly pale and Phelan was watching him closely.

"Thus," said Mercado, "Constance here got in touch with a lawyer—a lawyer, I regret to say, who had something of a reputation for getting in touch with men evading the law. Mr. Harkwell went into action."

I heard a sibilant intake of breath at my side. I turned to see Huerta, grim-lipped, glaring at Mercado.

"Mr. Harkwell went with Constance to Mexico," said Mercado, "as soon as the lawyer, through his many connections, had arranged to meet Widders, or Crothers."

"And did he meet him?" asked Jane Harkwell.

Mercado nodded. "He met him and was killed."

"But why should Mr. Crothers kill my uncle?"

Mercado smiled faintly. "Self defense."

The girl gasped. "You mean my uncle tried to kill Mr. Crothers?"

"Exactly. That was the only reason he and Constance went to Mexico."

"But why?"

"Once Crothers was definitely dead there was no further obstacle to the marriage. It's as easy as that."

"I don't quite get it," said Phelan.

"Neither do I," said Constance. "It's idiotic. I am not going to remain here to be insulted."

Without removing the toothpick from his mouth, Phelan said: "Sit down, bud."

Constance sat down.

"Let's make it clearer," said Mercado. "Constance and Harkwell were after Mrs. Crothers' millions. They wanted Crothers out of the way for obvious reasons. They traced him and went to Mexico to kill him. Harkwell left his hotel that night to meet him and do the job. However, Crothers was too good for him. He killed Harkwell before the lawyer could kill him.

"He left him in the Calle Niza, and our pal, Gomez, dragged him into the Embassy grounds and planted a gun in his hand to make it look like suicide."

A thought came to me. "And when Constance heard of it, of course, he yelled, 'Murder!' Then Crothers got in touch with him and they made a deal. Crothers would keep his mouth shut about being alive, would provide Huerta, here, to say he was dead and Constance could pay off when he got Mrs. Crothers' cash."

"You're largely right," said Mercado. "But you will recall I agreed a short time ago that Huerta was actually Crothers' best friend. Do you know how I happened to come to that conclusion?"

We looked at him expectantly.

"Because," said Mercado, "Huerta *is* Crothers, or Widders."

THERE WAS a sharp cry from Alicia Crothers. Huerta came to his feet. He fired a Spanish oath at Mercado, then added two more in English. His bass voice resounded through the room.

Alicia Crothers cried: "Harry! That's my husband. I'd know that voice anywhere! "

Jane Harkwell crossed the room and took the old lady's hand. Mercado continued.

"Both Crothers and Constance were afraid of a doublecross. Crothers couldn't get money from his wife without coming to the States. He was afraid to do that. Constance couldn't collect unless he could convince the old lady that Crothers was dead. So they came along together. If Constance crossed Crothers, he could stop the wedding. If Crothers tried to cross Constance, he could turn him in to the coppers. So he assumed the name 'Huerta' and they traveled together."

"Except," I said, "between Camaron and the Border."

"Ah," said Mercado, "that's what gave it away. Crothers left the train at Camaron. He reappeared in San Antonio. Why? Because he had no papers. He did not dare pass through the immigration office. He had a car ready, drove to the Border and simply waded across the Rio Grande at night."

I thought of something. "What about our private detective, Mendoza?"

"Crothers killed him. Mendoza was an old copper. Once he saw Huerta he knew he was Widders. He went down to Headquarters and checked Widders' crime. I learned that downtown. Obviously then he, too, sold out. He got hold of Widders and tried blackmail. Widders killed him."

The man known as Huerta said: "This is a stupid lie. I am neither Widders nor Crothers."

"That's an easy one," said Phelan. "We've got Widders' prints downtown. I don't care whether you're Crothers or not."

"We've got Crothers' prints, too," said Mercado. "In a safe, a safe that's never been opened in twenty-eight years, which has never been opened at all, save by Crothers, himself."

"I think that will do," said Phelan. "We'll take one for murder and the other for fraud, conspiracy and concealing criminal knowledge of murder. Come on, you two."

Alicia Crothers uttered a little gasp and fainted. Jane rushed toward the bedroom for smelling salts. Constance looked like a dead man.

As Phelan moved toward Huerta, the latter's hand moved with amazing rapidity to his hip. He pulled out a gun and slugged Phelan on the skull. Then he kicked out at Mercado's shin and was out of the room before I could move. The door slammed behind him before I was out of my chair.

Phelan recovered first, and brilliantly. He grabbed Constance, clicked a pair of handcuffs on him and clicked the other end of the cuffs onto the steam pipe. Then yelling to Mercado and me to follow, he took to his heels. The three of us charged out the door together.

We were lucky to find the elevator at our floor. As we went shooting down, inquiry revealed that Crothers must have used the stairs. In the hall the doorman hadn't seen him. That meant he must have used the back stairs.

We rushed out the service entrance of the building into the side street. We caught sight of Crothers speeding around the western corner. We charged after him, Mercado, coattails flying, in the lead, Phelan second and me about four lengths behind him in the rear.

At the corner, we saw Crothers duck into a doorway. We plunged along behind. We went through a dark corridor into a backyard. Crothers was on the top of a fence and fast disappearing.

Phelan's gun cracked once. We scrambled over the fence and I heard Mercado mutter: *"Dios,* my suit!" We landed jarringly on the other side and looked quickly around. Crothers was nowhere in sight.

There was a doorway before us, in front of which were a dozen garbage cans. A most unpleasant smell greeted our nostrils. Phelan plunged forward through the sickening stench. As we gained the doorway, we saw a kitchen, the filthiest kitchen I have ever seen in my life. And in the middle of it sprawled Crothers in a pool of grease. Doubtless, he had slipped and fallen as he was running through.

He sprang across the floor and barricaded himself behind a barrel of beer. We saw his gun barrel over the top of it. Beside me I heard Mercado hiccup. This time I didn't blame him.

The wooden floor on which we stood had a layer of grease an inch thick and in that grease was embedded the dirt of a decade. There were five uncovered garbage cans, filled to the hilt, on which were feasting a horde of the largest cockroaches I have ever seen.

A half naked, grimy looking man stood staring at us by a rusty, filthy stove. At a sink stood two more unwashed individuals dumping dishes into water that would have killed a typhus germ.

Phelan said: "Come out of there. There are three of us."

"Get out yourselves," said Crothers, "or you'll be three corpses."

"You asked for it," said Phelan and fired. His bullet ricocheted off the barrel. Two shots came from Crothers' gun. Mercado took a deep breath. He picked up a pot which hung nearby and hurled it at Crothers. And as Crothers ducked, he sprang. He vaulted the barrel easily and landed like a frog on Crothers' shoulder.

His hands seized the wrist of Crothers' gun hand. In another instant, Phelan and I were there, too. Crothers was soon disarmed and held firmly in the copper's grasp.

Phelan shot an admiring glance at Mercado. "Nice work," he said. "Very nice."

Mercado looked around the kitchen slowly. *"Dios,"* he said. "Let us get out of here! What sort of place is this?"

"This?" said Phelan. "Oh, it's the kitchen of some little chili joint that fronts on the avenue."

Mercado stared at him.

"Qué?" he shrieked. *"Qué dice?"*

I repeated what Phelan had said.

The greatest private detective in Mexico stared at me with bulging eyes. He muttered, *"Dios,"* twice, then fainted dead away.

IT WAS on the southbound train that I asked him: "Just when did you decide that Huerta was Crothers?"

He shrugged his shoulders and looked most melancholy. "I entertained the idea all along. However, you will recall that we overheard Constance and Crothers talking to the old lady one day and Crothers wasn't using his bass voice, which was most distinctive. He had raised it a full tone."

"So his wife wouldn't recognize him?"

"Precisely."

He lapsed into sad silence again. I said: "What's wrong? Didn't you enjoy the trip?"

He shook his head, said miserably: "I can't sleep. Nightmares. That kitchen. I shall not live two weeks."

A HOUND FOR MURDER

AT THE RISK OF HYDROPHOBIA, SEPTICEMIA AND AMEBIC DYSENTERY, MARIANO MERCADO DROPPED HIS BATTLE WITH BACTERIA TO SOLVE THE CASE OF THE MISSING MILLIONAIRE. MERCADO, WHO BECAME FAINT AT THE SIGHT OF DIRT, FACED THE MURDERER'S GUN WITHOUT A QUAVER. BUT IT WAS A GERM THAT FINALLY TOLD HIM OFF!

CHAPTER ONE
THE GERMLESS
WONDER

IT WAS a bright summer morning. The Mexican sun beat down bravely on the lush foliage of Chapultepec Park. High on a hill overlooking the lake stood the majestic ancient palace where once the ill-fated Maximilian and his empress had lived.

Mariano Mercado and I had breakfasted well and were permitting our digestions to work quietly as we sat on a bench beneath a bower of bougainvillea. The sole disturbing note to the serenity of the environment was Mercado's raiment.

His suit was a nice cross between bottle green and canary yellow. Its cut proclaimed his tailor a redoubtable individualist. His shoes were of two tones either of which would have caused an art critic to wince and his socks were of a blue which put the cloudless sky to shame.

His shirt was gray and if you think gray can be nothing more than a melancholy color, you don't know Mariano Mercado's haberdasher. However, the crescendo point of the entire ensemble was his tie. The cravat which encircled his rather scrawny throat was an admixture of every hue known to man, ancient and modern. It hit the eye like a baseball bat and left the observer blinking and shaken.

A hundred yards or so off to our right a group of workmen were busily engaged in applying a fresh coat of crimson paint to the bandstand. Before us the lake was crowded with boats and the sound of clashing oars and imprecation filled the air.

A well-dressed man sauntered down the walk, paused at our bench, then sat down on the end of it. Mercado was at the other end, a good six feet from the newcomer with me sitting between them. A sudden shudder coursed through his slight frame.

"*Dios,*" he muttered in a stricken tone. "Let us move to another bench. *Pronto!*"

I sidestepped and batted at it with the barrel of my gun.

The expression of horror on his chocolate-colored face was quite familiar to me—I knew what had caused it. I shot a hasty glance at the stranger.

He was a man of medium size, with an impressive mustache, the ends of which curled upward in the general direction of the *Pleiades*. His complexion was lighter than that of Mercado, making it easy to see the little network of pimples on his skin.

I turned my head back to Mercado but he had already risen and was twenty feet away, moving as fast as he could without actually breaking into a dog trot. I sighed, stood up and followed him.

He selected another seat, squatted on it and thrust an anxious hand in his pocket. He withdrew an atomizer and sprayed into his mouth some secret solution known only to himself and his pharmacist. He replaced the atomizer and dug a small bottle out of his pocket. This lotion he rubbed carefully over his hands and his face.

I said irritably: "What's the matter with you this time?"

"If you are fool enough to risk your life it is your own affair," he said coldly, "I have no intention of perishing of some ghastly disease."

"What disease?"

"I don't know. But you saw that *hombre's* face? You saw those hideous ulcers?"

"Ulcers!" I snorted. "They were barely perceptible. In all probability the man suffers from some allergy."

"Perhaps," said Mercado incredulously. "But I do not gamble with my life. Do you know how many millions of virulent virus can exist on the point of a pin?"

As a matter of fact I knew quite well. He had told me often enough. I possessed more health statistics than an insurance actuary. I had become a walking compendium of disease since I had thrown in my lot with Mariano Mercado.

He possessed the physical courage of an enraged lion— when he was faced with visible adversaries. I had seen him tackle an armed thug with his bare hands. I had seen him wirily wrench a knife from a man twice as big as himself who was bent on putting an end to the career of Mariano Mercado. But once he suspected the presence of a germ, he was the liliest-livered poltroon in all the world.

His array of lotions, medications and drugs with which to battle with the invisible hordes of bacteria cost him half of each peso he earned in his private detective business. The lengths to which he went to avoid all contact with anyone who had even a slight cold seemed weird even to a guy who knows several psychotics.

And now he sat on a park bench, thoroughly terrified by a stranger with a dozen pimples on his face, disseminating vital statistics into my reluctant ear.

IT WAS I who saw the *tourista* first. She was a fat woman with vast bosoms and thick bare arms. She was dressed in white and the inevitable camera was slung around her shoulders. She rounded a clump of trees some fifty yards from where we sat and even at that distance I could see that she was excited.

She grabbed the first pedestrian she met, seized his coat lapels and screamed something unintelligible at him. The victim, a little old gentleman taking his morning constitutional, stared at her, broke away and loped down the path.

The *tourista* kept on going. A boy and a girl passed her and she yammered at them. They too stared, then hurried on their way. When the woman was about twenty paces from us, I could see her white face and her gaping eyes.

She said aloud and apparently to Heaven: "Good Lord, is there no one in this benighted country who can speak English? Dead men lying all over the park and no one understands what I am talking about!"

Mercado and I exchanged glances. We rose simultaneously. Mercado bowed to her and said: "May we help, Madam?"

Her frightened eyes transfixed him. "Can you speak English?"

He could speak it infinitely better than she could but he forebore to tell her that. He said simply: "Yes."

"Well, there's a dead man back there. In the bushes. My string of pearls happened to break. One of them rolled into the bushes and I went in after it. Then I saw him. A hole in his head. He's dead. It's disgusting. Nothing like this could ever happen in Central Park!"

The New York Police Department could have refuted that remark but there was no use pressing the point. Mercado and I followed back in the direction whence she had come. We turned away from the lake and followed a narrower, less frequented path. On its left was a thick growth of bushes. The *tourista* pointed a be-ringed finger at the center of the foliage and said: "There! He's in there!"

I plunged into the bushes, Mercado at my heels and the *tourista* peering fearfully over our shoulders. Lying on its back, sombrero at its side, was the body of a man. Dead center in his forehead was an ugly crimson scar. He was clad in shabby blue pants and a dirty shirt. A pair of cheap *huaraches* covered his sockless feet.

Mercado and I stared at him for a moment. Then it came to me that a faint odd droning sound was pouring into my ears. It took me a moment to place it. Then I burst into laughter. The corpse was snoring.

I heard the *tourista* gasp behind me. Mercado bent down and shook the man. He opened his eyes, blinked twice, then came to his feet with the respectful air of a peon.

"But he *was* dead," cried the American woman. "I know he was dead."

The corpse shook his head and said: *"No digo Inglis."*

Mercado said in Spanish: "What are you doing here? What's that red stuff on your forehead?"

The man grinned. "Sleeping, *señor*. That is all. I was watching the bandstand painters and I got myself daubed with a little paint."

We stepped back out of the bushes to the footpath. The *tourista* was shaking her head emphatically. "Surely, I know a dead man when I see one."

"And," said Mercado, "how many dead men have you seen, *señora?*"

The woman shook her head and made a gesture which implied that she washed her well-manicured hands of the whole thing. Muttering, she took herself off in the direction of the park's exit.

At that moment I heard a footfall behind me and turned around to see the man who had driven Mercado off our original bench. He came to a sudden halt and glared like a headlight at our recently revivified corpse. The latter met his gaze for a moment, then dropped his eyes.

Mercado now caught sight of the new arrival. An expression of horror flitted across his face and he turned and walked up the path as quickly as his tiny feet would carry him. I was about to go after him when the pimpled individual said loudly: *"Hijo de perro. Cabrone!"*

He took a step forward and unleashed a hard left which took the other dead on the point of the jaw. He staggered backwards and fell. The pimpled man looked at his fallen adversary for a moment, then at me. He took a deep breath and to his heels almost in the same instant.

He raced away in the opposite direction to that taken by Mariano Mercado. I shrugged my shoulders and moved off myself, leaving our corpse flat on his back in precisely the same position as we had found him.

THE COMBINATION office and dwelling of Mariano Mercado was a model for any hospital. It was as sterile, as sanitary as a hundred pesos' worth of the most modern drugs could make it. It possessed neither curtains nor draperies. Such fripperies as these may have been pleasing to the eye but on the other hand they were, as Mercado said often and loudly, an engraved invitation to any homeless germ to move right in.

The white medicine chests in his bathroom held an array of bottles that would have impressed a stockholder in a chemical company. The top of his desk held the overflow, plus a few items, such as his atomizer, which were in constant demand.

The hour of the siesta was over. It was a little after four o'clock in the afternoon. I was glancing through the evening paper while Mercado pored over a medical report concerning the incidence of amebic dysentery in the state of Chihuahua.

I heard the footfalls on the stairway outside. A moment later the doorbell rang. I put down my paper, crossed the room to the foyer and opened it.

The moment I saw our visitor I knew he would not be welcome. It was the pimplyfaced man who had driven Mercado from his bench that morning, the man who had knocked out the sleeping peon. He said: "I wish to see the *señor* Mercado."

I led him into the living room and tactfully gestured toward the chair which was farthest removed from Mercado's desk. He sat down and removed his hat. Mercado looked up from his medical report, stared at the stranger and shuddered fearfully as he recognized him. His hand stretched out in a reflexive action and gripped a bottle of antiseptic. Only an innate courtesy prevented him from using it then and there.

"My name," said the stranger, "is Luis Mendoza. I saw you in Chapultepec Park this morning. I knew your face was familiar. Later I recalled having seen it in the newspapers. I knew then that you were Mariano Mercado, *detectivo particular.* I knew also you were the man I wanted. I wish to retain you, *señor.*"

Mercado was staring at the rash on the man's cheeks. He had a death grip on the bottle of antiseptic. He said in a nervous tone: "What is it you want me to do?"

"To find a man. I will pay you five hundred pesos if you can tell me what has become of Juan Ruiz."

"First," said Mercado, "the details."

Mendoza bowed. "Very well. Juan Ruiz is a friend of mine, my best friend. Our fathers stood shoulder to shoulder in the revolution. Juan and his brother, Pedro, inherited a valuable silver mine in the state of Guerrera. Pedro was always a spendthrift who devoted his days to dissipation and vice. His brother advanced him thousands of pesos. So much that he will be entitled to nothing from the mine for years to come. However, he still owns a fifty percent interest."

Mariano Mercado released the bottle of antiseptic long enough to make some sketchy notes on a scratch pad. Mendoza sighed and went on with his story.

"Recently, two attempts were made on Juan's life. He was shot at twice, each time from ambush while riding to and from the mine. He apparently had no enemies. He became badly worried, so he telephoned me. He wanted me to take charge of his property while he went away for a while. His nerves were upset because of the attempts on his life. When I spoke to him he sounded very much afraid. He made an appointment to meet me in Chapultepec Park last night."

Mercado nodded. "And he did not show up?"

"He did not. I waited until after midnight. Then I went home to bed. I returned to the park first thing this morning. It was then that I saw you. It was then, also, that I saw the sleeping peon."

"The *hombre* you slugged in the jaw," I said. "And why did you do that?"

"I lost my head. But when I saw him I was certain he had something to do with the troubles of my friend, Juan."

"But why should he have anything to do with Juan Ruiz?"

"Because, *señor*," Mendoza spoke very softly, "because that peon you found sleeping in the bushes was Pedro Ruiz, the brother of my friend."

I glanced over at Mercado. In my book this was either a very large coincidence or there was something fishy here which did not meet the naked eye—my eyes at least. Mercado wore a thoughtful expression as if he was on the verge of an answer.

Finally he said: "And you will pay me five hundred pesos if I tell you what has become of your friend?"

"*Sí, señor.*"

"Then," said Mercado slowly, "I think I can tell you."

Mendoza gaped at him. For that matter, so did I.

I said: "You mean you know the answer right now?"

"I think so," said Mercado again. "However, for five hundred pesos, it is better to make sure. Latham, you will return immediately to the park. You will question those workmen. You will find out if there was a parked car which had broken down anywhere near the bandstand when they came to work this morning."

I stood up somewhat puzzled. "Is that all you want me to find out?"

"That's all."

I shrugged and left the room, leaving Mercado alone with the man of the pimply face. I knew what he was going through for those five hundred pesos. It was like leaving anyone else to face an artillery barrage.

I took a taxi out to the park, dutifully asked my questions, jotted down the answers and hailed another cab for the return trip. I was back in Mercado's flat well within the hour.

THEY WERE sitting in exactly the same positions as when I had left them. Mercado looked up as I entered and said: "Well, was there a car?"

"There was a car," I said. "It was parked when the men came to work. Shortly after that another car drove up. Two men got out and repaired the first car. The second car drove off."

"And what then?"

I shrugged. "That was about all I could find out. The other car, I presume, drove off too. But I don't see what all this has to do with the disappearance of Juan Ruiz."

"You don't?" said Mercado with a faint tilt of his eyebrows. "Well, Juan Ruiz was in the car which had been repaired."

I looked at him incredulously. Mendoza said excitedly: "Then where is Juan Ruiz now?"

"I am not a theologist," said Mariano Mercado.

It took some twenty seconds for this remark to penetrate my skull. When it did, I said: "You mean he's dead?"

"He is dead," said Mariano Mercado, "and I have earned five hundred pesos."

Luis Mendoza ran a hand over his pimples. He said: "Would you kindly explain this, *señor?*"

"*Por favor, señor,*" I said not without irony. I had seen him pull some odd rabbits out of some oddly assorted hats in my time, but I didn't see how, on the basis of the facts, he was so certain that Juan Ruiz was a corpse.

"I am a man of fixed prejudices," said Mercado, "and I hate to admit that a *tourista* could be right about anything. But she was."

"You mean she actually *did* see a dead man?"

"She did. She saw Juan Ruiz."

"She did not. She saw his brother, Pedro." Mercado shook his head. "*We* saw Pedro," he said gently. "*She* saw Juan."

Mendoza and I both waited patiently for further enlightenment.

"I am not a strong believer in coincidence," said Mercado. "Juan is supposed to be in Chapultepec Park on Wednesday evening. On Thursday morning his brother is discovered there sleeping in the bushes, with a spot of red paint on his forehead. It is a strange place to get smeared with paint. There was none on his hands, none on his clothes."

A faint light flickered for me now. "Go on," I said.

"Very well. Suppose someone is aware of the fact that Juan Ruiz is to be in the park on Wednesday evening. We will assume it is the same person who already has tried twice to kill him. He waylays him in the park and does what he has already failed to do before. He has a car with him in which to carry off the body. But at the crucial moment the car breaks down. What does he do?"

"Well," I said, "he fixes the car and gets the body away as soon as he can."

"And if he can't fix it himself?"

"He calls a garage."

"Not after ten o'clock in Mexico, he doesn't. There aren't any garages open. He must wait until morning."

"So," I said, picking it up, "he can't just sit there with a body in his lap until dawn when he'll be observed, so he drags the corpse into the bushes."

"Right. And at nine o'clock or so he calls a garage, they send a repairman who fixes the car. Now, in all probability, he intends to leave the body where it is and pick it up at night when it will be safer. But a *tourista* blunders onto his body, just at the time when the car is fixed up again."

"All right. But why doesn't he just run away and leave the body there?"

"For some reason," said Mariano Mercado, "he does not want it known that Juan Ruiz is dead. He doesn't even want to gamble by taking the body away and letting the *tourista* howl that she saw a corpse in the bushes a few moments before. That would interest the *policia* and our killer, for some reason, still unknown, does not want the *policia* interested in the case. So, he simply daubs the forehead of Juan's brother, Pedro, with red paint and has him pretend to be asleep. It is now simply a matter of a hysterical female tourista who has made a comical mistake."

"You just remarked," I told him, "that you were not a strong believer in coincidence. Is it not an incredible coincidence that Juan's brother happened to be there just when he was needed?"

"*Valgame Dios!*" said Mercado. "You have the mentality of a retarded goat. In view of what Señor Mendoza has just told us, is it not most likely that the ne'er-do-well brother may well have been in the plot?"

HE TURNED to Mendoza. "*No es verdad, señor?* And have I earned five hundred pesos?"

"*Creo que si,*" said Mendoza, reaching for his wallet. He counted out five hundred pesos in creased and dirty bills. I gathered them up knowing quite well that Mercado would not have touched them with a gun at his head. Money, he had told me often enough, was a favorite breeding place for bacteria.

"And now," said Mendoza, and there was anger in his voice, "would you care to earn another thousand pesos, *señor?*"

"I was rather waiting for this," said Mercado. "You want to find out who killed your friend?"

"And why."

Mariano Mercado nodded. "Very well. First, tell me where this Ruiz mine is situated."

"In the mountains between Taxco and Iguala. The mine office is in Taxco."

"Leave your address with the *señor* Latham and I will get in touch with you."

I jotted down Mendoza's address and he left leaving a trail of repetitious Spanish thank-yous behind him. The instant the door closed behind him, Mercado uncorked the bottle.

He atomized and sterilized himself. He sprayed the chair on which Mendoza had sat. He swallowed two pink pills. Then for the first time in two hours he relaxed.

"A man like that should be quarantined," he said.

"Why? He's only got some slight skin rash. He—"

Mercado leaned forward and brandished a forefinger under my nose. "Do you know what a skin rash might lead to? Do you realize—"

This was a variation on a speech I had heard at least three thousand times since our association had begun. I essayed to cut him off.

"It seems to me," I interrupted, "that you've just picked up a thousand pesos in the gutter."

He dropped the health lecture and said with some indignation. "What do you mean by that?"

"Well, you've been offered a thousand pesos to find out who killed Juan Ruiz and why. Since the brother will doubtless inherit the mine, since the brother was apparently on the scene at the time of the murder—always provided your prime theory is correct—even the mind of a retarded goat can figure out that your villain is Pedro. It's merely a matter of finding him and assembling some evidence."

Mercado shook his head slowly. There was a doleful expression on his face.

"It won't be that easy, Latham. I do not deny that Pedro is mixed up in this but it's hardly a matter of simple murder. If it were, Pedro would have killed his brother and put as many kilometers between himself and the corpse as possible. He would not have loafed around all day at the murder scene. He would have gone out of his way to arrange an alibi which, I regret to say, is all too easy to do in my country."

I thought it over, then advanced a daring hypothesis. "Of course," I said, "you may be wrong. Juan Ruiz may be alive. All you have is a pretty abstract theory, you know."

"Well," he said, "the first move is obvious. We'll check the Taxco office. See if they think they know where Juan is. Telephone them. Also see if you can find out the value of the mine. The Federal Department of Mines will have that. There's no rush. Let me know in the morning."

By now it was time for me to return to my hotel and change my clothes for dinner. I bade Mercado farewell and went on my way.

CHAPTER TWO
WHEN IS A CORPSE NOT
A CORPSE

I SPENT an evening dabbling lightly in the flesh-pots along the Paseo Reforma, got home at two o'clock only mildly cock-eyed and slept the sleep of the just. In the morning I put through a long distance call to Taxco, and visited the Department of Mines.

I arrived at Mercado's with my report a little before noon. I was glad that he had already completed every detail of his morning toilet. The bottles on his desk had been used and tightly recorked. He was bathed, shaved, atomized, antisepticized and thoroughly disinfected.

He sat behind his desk perusing the morning paper, *Excelsior*. He was not reading the political news, nor the charts of yesterday's racing at the Hippodrome, nor the scores of the *beisbol* game in Señor Pasquel's stadium. No. He had discovered an article on the malarial mosquito. And he was giving it every ounce of concentration he had.

He looked up as I came in. "Latham," he said in grave and hollow tones, "listen to what this article—"

This time I didn't worry. I knew I had something that would keep him from a sanitation lecture for a little while.

"You listen to me," I said. "I've done some checking for you. That Ruiz mine outside of Taxco is worth something over two million pesos at present silver prices. At least that's what it sold for yesterday."

He blinked slowly and temporarily dropped the matter of the malarial mosquito.

"It was sold yesterday?"

"To an American. For two million, two hundred and fifty thousand pesos. His name is Apthorp and he's staying at the Hotel Los Arcos. Juan Ruiz' secretary is there also and Juan himself is registered though he wasn't in his room when I checked."

"That," said Mercado, "fails to amaze me."

He tapped a thoughtful and sterilized finger on the desk top.

He said: "How was it sold? What were the terms of the sale? How could it be sold without the presence of the principal owner, Juan Ruiz?"

I shrugged my shoulders. "There are a couple of guys over at the Los Arcos who doubtless could answer those questions. I can't."

Mariano Mercado stood up. Today he was wearing his blue suit but it was not a blue that you have seen in the window of any tailor shop in all the world. It was a brighter blue than the prism ever suspected. His shirt was yellow and his tie matched his socks which were utterly ineffable.

He selected a fawn-colored hat, donned it and said: *"Vamanos. A Los Arcos."*

J. Wellington Apthorp was a stereotype. He was more typical of the American business man than anyone has a right to expect. His hair was thin and receding so fast you could almost see it go. A pair of shrewd blue eyes stared out from behind a pair of black-rimmed glasses. His clothes were conservatively cut and both their style and color made

them seem shroud-like next to Mercado's blazing haber-
dashery.

His demeanor was brisk but pleasant. His manner was
that of a man who counts every minute and every dollar.
We were admitted to his suite, offered cigars and chairs.

Mercado showed his credentials and said in his precise
and perfect English: *"Señor,* I am working on a case for a
most important client, a member of the Federal Government. I need some assistance from you."

Of course that statement was a blatant lie. Mercado was
using it in order to obtain what information he wanted.
When a foreigner buys property in Mexico he finds himself
hedged in by various complicated laws which require the
services of at least four lawyers and all the friends at court
that can be assembled. Since Apthorp was about to engage
in mining he would think twice about rebuffing a private
detective who was working for a government official.

"Certainly," said Apthorp. "Anything at all."

"First," said Mercado, "I understand that you have
bought a mine in the state of Guerrero."

Apthorp nodded. "Signed the final papers yesterday."

"What time yesterday?"

"Early. About eight o'clock in the morning."

"May I ask who signed those papers other than yourself?"

"The mine owners. The Ruiz brothers."

Mercado's eyebrows approached the ceiling. *"Both* of
them? Pedro and Juan?"

"Naturally. They are the joint owners of the mine. How
could I buy the mine without their signatures?"

I grinned. It wasn't often I nailed Mercado in an error.
But it was obvious that if Juan Ruiz had signed a paper

in this hotel room at eight o'clock yesterday morning, he could not have been a corpse hidden in a bush in Chapultepec Park.

Mercado sighed. "Was anyone else present at this contract signing?"

"Yes. Mr. Drayton. He's an American. He is the Ruiz general manager."

"And has the money been paid?"

"Twenty percent of it. The rest is to be paid into the Ruiz bank within thirty days. Then I will take over the property."

Mercado sighed again. I could see he wasn't very happy.

"Would you mind if I asked Mr. Drayton to come up here? I understand he is registered at this hotel."

Apthorp reached for the telephone. "Certainly. And would you care to see Mr. Juan Ruiz? He, too, is registered here."

"You may try him," said Mercado. He glanced at me and added stubbornly: "But he won't be in."

IN THAT, at least, he was right. Juan Ruiz' room did not answer. After a few minutes there was a knock at the door and Apthorp admitted Drayton.

Drayton was a man of medium height with a sunburned face and narrowed eyes. Apthorp introduced him to us. After he was seated, Mercado said: "I just want to be sure that both Juan and Pedro Ruiz were in this room yesterday between eight and half past in the morning."

"Sure they were," said Drayton. "They signed the sales contract."

"You know both brothers?"

"Sure, I do."

Mercado sighed again. It was obvious that he didn't like this at all. He tried again.

"Were both the men here at the same time?"

Apthorp shook his head. "No. Pedro came in about ten minutes after Juan had signed and left."

"You see," explained Drayton, "there was bad blood between them. They didn't want to see each other if it could be avoided, so we avoided it."

Some of Mercado's melancholy seemed to leave him. "Tell me, Señor Apthorp, did you find they looked very much alike?"

Apthorp shook his head. "Not at all. Juan has a mustache, is taller and extremely well dressed. The brother is dressed like a peon, clean-shaven and stooped. I wouldn't have known they were brothers if I hadn't been told."

"And you," said Mercado to Drayton, "you saw both men yesterday?"

"Sure I did."

Mariano Mercado passed a hand over his forehead. "All I can say," he said, "is that I am baffled. Thank you, *señores* and *bueno dias.*"

He turned on his heel and left the room. I trotted along after him.

We got out into the street in silence and I followed Mercado into a *cantina*. He sat at the bar and ordered a *habanero*. I said, *"Dos,"* to the bartender and sat down beside him.

Mariano Mercado wiped the glass carefully with a gleaming handkerchief before he tilted the bottle over it. He sighed, lifted the *habanero* and drank it. He performed the same rite three times. I went right along with him.

He set the glass on the bar finally and said: "I think we shall visit the *señor* Mendoza. Perhaps he can clear up some of the questions in my mind."

We hailed a taxicab and journeyed to the hotel of the *señor* Mendoza. It was a third rate hostelry over near the colorful Juarez market. A thin and dour-faced clerk informed us that the *señor* Mendoza occupied room number 118.

There was no elevator. We climbed up a narrow staircase over a worn carpet. We walked down a dim corridor and halted before a door.

I was about to knock when Mercado, whose eyes were those of a precocious eagle, said: *"Mira!* Look down there."

I looked down at the dingy carpeting which his forefinger indicated. I failed to see anything.

"What is it?"

"There is a liquid seeping from beneath the door."

"Probably water. Maybe he upset a glass or something."

"It is not the color of water," said Mercado gravely. He paused for a moment and added: "It is the color of blood."

Then he put his hand on the knob and turned it. The door, it appeared, was unlocked. Mariano Mercado and I walked into the room. I took a single glance at Mendoza's huddled figure on the floor and slammed the door shut behind me.

In the next instant Mercado and myself were on our knees beside Mendoza. He wore no coat and there was a red stain on his shirt in the region of his heart. There was a trail of blood from the window to the door indicating that he had been shot down on the other side of the room and had crawled across it. He was indubitably dead.

There was a pencil on the floor near the body and in his left hand was clutched an unsealed envelope. I took the envelope from his hand and examined it. It was addressed to Mariano Mercado.

Without speaking I handed it to Mercado. He put his fingers inside it and withdrew a thousand peso note. Scrawled across its face was some scribbled writing.

Here is the fee. Now find out also—

Mercado sighed. He stared at the pimply face of the dead man and he did not appear horrified. Apparently he had even forgotten his fear of handling money, for he held on to the bank note as he looked at the dead man.

He said at last in a voice, deeply moved: "He is an honest man, Latham. Even as he died he thought of my fee."

"And revenge," I said. "He doubtless wanted to make sure you'd get the guy who killed him."

He glanced down at his tiny hand, noted that he still held the thousand peso note and shuddered.

"Here," he said, thrusting it at me, "bank this."

He stood up and thoroughly scrubbed his hands in the wash basin.

I put the money in my pocket and said: "What do we do now? Call the gendarmes?"

He shook his head. "They'll find him soon enough and it is better that *el coronel* Gomez does not know that we have any knowledge of it."

That was true, enough. *El coronel* Gomez of the local police was no bosom friend of Mercado's.

"All right," I said. "What do we do? Just put the thousand pesos in the bank and forget the whole thing?"

He regarded me with disapproval. "Our client may be dead but the work is paid for. We shall find out who killed him. We shall also find out who killed Juan Ruiz."

"How?" I said very practically.

He didn't answer me. He opened the door and went out into the hall. I followed him, closing the door carefully behind me. We took a taxi back to Mercado's place.

THERE HE washed thoroughly with disinfectant and used his atomizer. Then he sat down in his sterilized chair behind his sterilized desk and heaved a weary sigh.

"It seems to me," I observed, "that we're up against a blank wall. Your original theory, obviously, was incorrect. We have nothing to go on."

"Oh, yes, we do," he said. "First, telephone that Apthorp and find out the address of Pedro Ruiz. He must have given it when he signed the contract. I think I shall ask him some questions."

He went back into his reveries as I used the telephone. I obtained the information and wrote it down on a scratch pad which I pushed over in front of him.

As he looked at it I heard footsteps coming up the stairs.

I opened the door and a voice, harsh and completely un-Mexican, said: "You ain't Mercado, are you, bud?"

I said that I was not. The visitor pushed roughly past me. He said: "I want to see Mercado."

He walked into the living room and leaned against the door jamb. I looked him over in the bright sunlight that came through Mercado's curtainless window.

Compared with anyone else than Mercado himself, our visitor's clothes would have seemed loud. He wore a pin-striped blue suit which fitted him tightly. His shirt was midnight blue and his tie matched. His shoes were bright yellow, his socks were the same color.

He was a man of about thirty. His face was absolutely white and his black eyes were half shut. I knew his type quite well. He was one of the mob boys. Probably, I guessed, from Chicago. He was tough and bloodless. From the dilation of his pupils I imagined he would have preferred a shot of heroin to a Scotch and soda.

He jerked his head in Mercado's direction and said: "You speaka da English?"

Mercado flushed. "I speak English if that's what you're asking."

"Good. Then it ought to be easy for you to understand me."

Mercado looked at him curiously. He was of a type with which Mariano Mercado was not familiar. He said icily, "I do not anticipate any difficulty in following your vocabulary, *señor*. What is it you wish to say?"

"My name," said the gunsel, "is Sammy Renault."

"Are we supposed to be familiar with it?" I asked.

"You would be if you hung around the Midwest. I got something of a rep up there."

"As what?" I said. "A pillar of the church?"

"Don't be a wise guy, chum. What I have to say is for this Mercado, not you."

"Well, say it."

"O.K." He fixed Mercado with his little black eyes. He opened the side of his mouth slightly and two harsh words dripped out.

"Lay off."

Apparently, Mercado had overplayed his hand a trifle when he had assumed he would have no difficulty in following Sammy Renault's vocabulary. His eyebrows lifted themselves and he stared at the gunman inquiringly.

"Lay off?" he repeated. "What does this mean?"

Sammy sighed in the manner of a man whose patience is being tried.

"Lay off. Keep your nose out. Don't be a buttinsky. Or else."

Mercado, who knew more English words than any American I had ever met, did not understand any of these. I stepped into the conversation.

"What is it you want him to lay off?"

"Whatever it was he was doing for Mendoza. He is also to keep his mouth shut."

"About what?"

"About anything he might know."

"And what does the 'or else' imply?"

Sammy Renault's lips became a thin vicious line. He looked at me through his half-closed lids.

"Listen," he said, "if a guy can get away with murder in Chicago, it's a cinch he can get away with it in Mexico. Mexico ain't tough. The cops ain't tough and it's easy to hide in the hills. Now, do you know what I mean by 'or else'?"

Now I knew and I said so.

"O.K.," said Sammy. He jerked a thumb in Mercado's direction. "So tell him and he'll know too."

I put it into the language Mercado would comprehend.

"He says that you're to stop working for Mendoza, that you're to keep your mouth shut if you know anything and that he'll kill you if you don't."

For a moment anger flashed in Mariano Mercado's eyes. He opened his mouth and I expected wrathful words. But he closed his lips again without speaking.

Then he said quite politely: "I need five minutes to think this over."

"Take half a day," said Sammy. "But be sure you decide right."

MERCADO LOOKED at him for a long time. Sammy still lounged in the doorway. He took a jackknife from his pocket, opened a murderous blade and proceeded to pare his nails.

From time to time he raised his slotted gaze and looked at Mercado. On each occasion that he did so, Mercado drummed his fingers nervously on the desk and registered timidity. This circumstance caused me some surprise. Of course, Mercado lived in deadly fear of bacteria but I had never seen him even mildly afraid of any tough guy that ever lived.

At last he said hesitantly: "I would like to discuss this privately with my assistant. Then I shall be able to tell you what course I can pursue."

Sammy Renault waved the jackknife deprecatingly. "I'm a patient man," he said. "Take all the time you want."

Mercado signalled to me and I followed him into the gleaming, germless bathroom. He closed the door cautiously.

"I don't blame you for being nervous," I said. "I know the type. He's a tough boy. A killer."

Mercado snapped his fingers and uttered a magnificent "Pouf!" He added: "I am not afraid of him. I am lulling him into a sense of false security. Now, listen. Where is our car?"

The coupé was in the garage around the corner and I told him so.

"All right. You have the address of Pedro Ruiz. How long will it take you to drive there?"

"Through Mexican traffic, say, twenty minutes."

"That will do. You will drive there at top speed the instant the gangman has gone."

"Gunman," I said.

He ignored me. "Within a short time after you have arrived at Pedro's home, he will leave. You will conceal yourself and wait outside. When he leaves you will follow him. When he arrives at his destination, you will endeavor to keep an eye on him and also telephone me telling me where you are. Do you understand?"

"I understand. But why? And how far is he going? And—"

He held up a silencing hand. "Later. There is no time for talk now. I must return and speak to this gangman."

"Gunman," I said, but he was already on his way to the living room.

He resumed his seat at the desk. Sammy Renault closed his knife and replaced it in his pocket. He said: "Well?"

"I have decided that this is all no affair of mine," said Mercado.

Sammy nodded and smiled bleakly. "A wise decision," he said. "It'll save us both a lot of trouble."

"But," said Mariano Mercado, "I must point out to you that it makes very little difference whether or not I quit the case. For, you see, the body is gone."

For the first time since he had entered the room Sammy's eyes opened wide. He said harshly: "What do you mean by that?"

Mercado spread his palms. "Simply that the body has been taken. And without the body you're in difficulties. At best there will be an investigation and it'll take a long time before there is any profit on the deal."

I hadn't the slightest idea what he was talking about. Sammy apparently did. "How do you know this?" he snarled.

"Mendoza told me."

"Then who took it? Where is it?"

Mercado spread his palms again. "He did not tell me that."

Sammy swore explosively. He slammed his right fist into the open palm of his left hand and swore again. Then he turned abruptly and raced from the room. I heard his heavy footfalls diminuendo down the stairway.

Mercado said: *"Vayase!* And quickly. There is no time to lose!"

I galloped down the stairs after Sammy. I raced around the corner to the garage and jumped into our coupé. I drove out into the streaming and chaotic traffic and headed for the address which Pedro Ruiz had given when he signed the contract.

CHAPTER THREE
MAD DOGS AND
MEXICANS

IT WAS a dilapidated three-story rooming house set a few feet back from the street. A rusted iron fence surrounded it and there was a tired palm tree standing in a weedy garden. Parked directly in front of it was a small sedan.

I parked my car on the corner, climbed out and stood behind it, peering through the window to the door of Pedro Ruiz' house. I remained in that position for some twenty minutes.

Then the door opened and Sammy Renault emerged. Accompanying him was Pedro and a mongrel dog about thirty percent terrier. Pedro was, I noticed, rather better dressed than when we had seen him in Chapultepec Park. He wore a dark business suit and shoes instead of *huaraches*.

They got into the sedan and set off to the south. I climbed back into the coupé and followed along.

I knew quite well that following Mercado's instructions would not be easy. The traffic in Mexico City is chaotic. The Sunday drivers are out every day and each man at a wheel is a thorough-going individualist.

However, I managed to keep the sedan in sight until we moved out into the suburbs and after that it looked somewhat easier. It appeared as if they were headed toward the

Ruiz mine. They took the road to Xochimilco, then continued on toward Cuernavaca and Taxco.

I cruised along after them. They drove speedily but there wasn't much traffic and I had no trouble keeping them in sight. My present worry was the fact that dusk was coming down and that it was going to be harder sticking to their tail in darkness.

On the other side of Cuernavaca, they braked before a restaurant and went inside, leaving the dog locked in the car. I figured that they were going to eat and that would give me enough time to call Mercado with a preliminary report.

I found a phone booth at a gas station and put through the call. I told Mercado where I was and in which direction we were headed.

He said: "Good. Write down the number of the booth you're in. I'll come out right away. When you reach your destination, phone me there. At least, I'll be part way to wherever we're going. And don't lose them."

I hung up, bought some *tacos* from a street vendor and washed it down with a bottle of beer. Then I got back in the car and waited for my quarry.

They came out shortly afterwards and the sedan moved on to the west. After a moment, so did my coupé.

The night came down over the Taxco mountains and the sedan turned off the main road about fifteen kilometers before we reached the historical old Borda silver mine. We bounced over a rutted dirt road, through a tiny hamlet of adobe houses.

Now, I permitted them to pick up quite a lead on me. Apparently they hadn't yet suspected that they were being followed. On this deserted, trafficless road it would become obvious if I remained in sight.

I slowed down to almost nothing and switched off my headlights. I drove with care, keeping my eyes on their tail light. Suddenly, it glowed a deeper red as the brakes were applied. I came to a full stop, pulled off the road into the bushes at its side and got out of the car.

The lights of their car went out completely. I heard the distant bark of their dog as he yapped happily at his freedom from the constricting limits of the sedan.

A moment later a light flickered a little to the left of the spot where the sedan had halted. I took my .38 from its shoulder holster and moved forward on foot.

Just then a faint new moon came gently over the top of the mountains to the west. It enabled me to see the dim outlines of their car up ahead and a larger bulk to its left. This second object was a house which apparently was built right up against the side of a hill.

I made my way along the edge of the road as silently as possible. As I drew near I saw a ramshackle, ancient adobe house whose back had been built flush up against the hillside. There were three small, high windows, following the fashion of Spanish colonial architecture peculiar to this region and a single door which faced the road beyond what had once been a garden and was now a lush tangle of trees, Spanish moss and shrubbery.

After observing these things, I went back to my car, praying that the *pueblo* which we had just come through boasted a telephone.

It did, though I had to route the local storekeeper out of bed and bribe him with ten pesos to let me use it.

I got Mercado at Cuernavaca and told him precisely where I was. He instructed me to return to the house and watch, to follow immediately if Sammy and Pedro left.

I went back to the house. I didn't believe I was going to have any more tracking to do that day. Kerosene lamps flickered inside the house and it seemed certain that the two of them intended to spend the night where they were.

Not that this made me very happy. I'd have to sit outside under a tree alone waiting until Mariano Mercado came up with more instructions.

I DID exactly that for a while then boredom and curiosity overcame me. I had no idea what Mercado was up to, nor for that matter what Sammy and Pedro were cooking. I decided to see if I could find out.

I went up to the house on stealthy feet. I maneuvered myself under one of the windows, then elevated myself on tiptoe and peered inside. I saw a rudely furnished room containing a rickety table, three broken-down chairs and a door which argued there was another room in the house.

Sammy was sitting at the table, scowling. Pedro bent over, lighting a lantern. The dog scratched up against the door and whined.

"Let that damned dog out," said Sammy. "He's getting on my nerves."

I noticed that Pedro, who could not speak English in Chapultepec Park seemed to understand it well enough now. Before I could move, he threw the front door open. The mongrel bounded out into the garden, then pulled up short.

I cursed for having left myself this wide open. The dog glared at me then barked frantically. Sammy sprang up from his seat and an automatic was in his hand.

I turned and faced the dog holding my .38 in fingers which were none too steady. The dog growled and sprang. I sidestepped and batted at it with the barrel of my gun.

I missed, and in that moment both Sammy and Pedro were facing me. Pedro held a knife in throwing position and Sammy's automatic was aimed at my heart in a most professional manner.

After completing my futile pass at the mongrel, the muzzle of my own gun was pointing at the adobe wall. Thus, when Sammy said, "Drop that gat, chum," I did so.

Pedro picked up my fallen gun and Sammy dragged me roughly inside. He threw me into one of the creaking chairs and slammed the door. He kept his automatic dead on my heart and said from the side of his mouth: "Wise guy, huh?"

I decided it was politic not to answer. I certainly did not feel like a wise guy. I felt like an egregious idiot. Whatever Mercado had planned, I had quite probably messed it all up. Not to mention the fact that I considered my own life was, at the moment, hanging by a thread.

All I could do was pray that Mercado and the Marines arrived in time.

"What do you guys think you're pulling?" said Sammy. "Are you trying to cross me?"

Since I didn't know what we were pulling, I couldn't tell him. He glared at me through his narrowed lids, then said abruptly to Pedro: "Get outside and see if it's there. We'll attend to this guy in a little while."

Pedro nodded. He picked up the lantern and went outside. Sammy, the automatic and I sat in silence.

Then suddenly from the darkness outside came some sharp words in Spanish. I heard an oath, then Mercado's familiar incisive tones. There was a yell and the crackle of two shots. An instant later Pedro raced into the house, breathless, slamming the door behind him. A bullet pinged up against the panel a second later.

Sammy stood up. His attention for a moment was removed from me.

"Mercado!" I yelled at the top of my voice. "I'm in here."

His voice came out of the night. "Is the gangman there?"

"Gunman," I yelled. "Yes!"

"That is good."

What was good about it I couldn't see. Sammy scowled at me and said: "Keep your mouth shut or I'll blast you." He lifted his voice and shouted to Mercado. "Come in and get me, spig."

"Oh, no," cried Mercado. "You come out."

"And get blasted in the doorway?" said Sammy. "Am I crazy?"

"You'll have to come out sometime," said Mercado. "And I can wait."

There was a long silence as all parties considered the situation. As I saw it, it was an absolute stalemate. If Mercado essayed to force an entrance single-handed, he would doubtless be killed. For that matter, so would I.

On the other hand if Pedro and Sammy attempted to leave the house by its only exit, Mercado, no mean marksman, would simply pick them off as they stepped outside the door.

Moreover, it was impossible for Mercado to go for help. Once he left, the pair in the house could make an easy getaway.

Sammy glanced over at me and sighed. It was evident that he had reached the same conclusions as I had.

He kept his gun on me and spoke to Pedro, "Was it there?"

"Sí. It was there."

Sammy looked at me. He said, "Wise guy," again from the corner of his mouth. He added: "Now I see what that little monkey was trying to pull."

"So," said Pedro Ruiz in broken English, "what is it we do now?"

"We got to get out of here," said Sammy Renault, "before that monkey out there can get the coppers."

"He can't go for the *policia*," said Pedro, "without letting us get away."

"Damn it," said Sammy, "we can't all sit around here for the rest of our lives. Stand away from that door and push it open a bit. See if the monkey's still there."

Pedro put his body against the wall, stretched out his arm and moved the door so that a tiny beam of light shone out into the garden. There was a sudden report and splinters of wood ripped from the panel.

"He's there," said Sammy grimly. "And he ain't a bad shot."

The night wore on. Once every hour Sammy ordered Pedro to open the door in order to ascertain that Mercado was still on sentry go. A well placed bullet always answered his question.

Sammy never relaxed his vigilance over me. Just before dawn he cursed and said: "It's going to be worse in daylight."

Pedro looked up suddenly. "No," he said. *"No es verdad,* I have an idea. Come with me into the bathroom, I shall tell you."

"I can't leave this joker here."

"You can tie him up."

Sammy considered this idea and found it good. Pedro produced a line of stout cord from somewhere and I was secured to the ancient chair on which I sat. Sammy and Pedro went into the other room.

I heard a murmur of conversation. The mongrel, already having betrayed me, was now prepared to make friends. He rubbed up against my knee and wagged his tail happily. I suspected he was full of fleas and did not relish his attention.

A little later the gray dawn came up and Sammy and Pedro emerged from the bathroom.

"All right," said Sammy, "we'll try it but I still think it's nuts."

"No," said Pedro, "it is a well known fact all over Mexico City."

"Wait till it's a little lighter and well try it. Is the monkey still out there?"

Pedro went through his door-opening routine once again and another bullet attested to the fact that the "monkey" was still there.

THE BRIGHT sun climbed up into the brilliantly blue sky and I wondered what strategy the enemy was about to use. I also wondered what was going on in Mercado's head. He wasn't the sort of guy who just sat down and let things happen to him.

"O.K.," said Sammy Renault, "get started."

Pedro bent down and opened a cheap suitcase which he had apparently brought with him. He took from it a shaving brush and one of those celluloid toilet sets affected by travellers. Then he went into the bathroom. In the doorway he turned and whistled to the mongrel. He snapped his fingers and said: *"Aqui, perro."* The dog wagged its tail and ran to him. He shut the bathroom door behind them both.

By this time my curiosity developed into complete bewilderment. Sammy kept his head away from the windows. Mercado, I knew, was well covered by the shrubbery and trees.

Then Pedro flung the door open and yelled to Sammy: "All right, open the front door."

Sammy stood to one side, turned the knob and flung the door open. I caught a swift flash of the mongrel leaping past me to the threshold. He was slavering. His muzzle was covered with white foam.

If I could have achieved complete objectivity in that moment I would have laughed. But I didn't. Pedro, aware, like most of Mexico, of Mercado's hypochondriac fears, had plastered shaving soap over the mongrel's muzzle and unleashed him on the little detective. I knew quite well what would happen.

From outside came a sudden shriek of terror. Sammy lifted his head gingerly and peered through the window. He turned around again and blinked in amazement. He said: "I never would have believed it. Come on, Pedro, quick!"

They flung open the front door and raced out toward their car. Through the doorway I had a perfect view of the ignominy of Mariano Mercado. He was racing like a deer across a wide uneven field at the far side of the dirt road. Behind him, enjoying the game, ran the dog, leaving flecks of shaving soap behind him.

Mercado was headed toward a gnarled and ancient tree which was now some fifty yards away from him. He stumbled once and fell. The dog gained on him at every step. Down the road I heard the sound of a car starting and knew Sammy and Pedro were on the last lap of their getaway.

Mercado reached the tree a bare step ahead of the dog. He scrambled up it like a man in deadly fear of his life, which, not to put too fine a point upon it, he was.

The dog leaped playfully, scratching its forepaws on the trunk. Mercado gained the first crotch of the tree and sat there an exhausted and terrified man.

I swung my chair around and banged it against the wall. Using my body to move it, I smashed it three times against the hard adobe. On the last try it broke into three pieces. I extricated myself from the rope and dashed out to the tree where Mercado sat.

The mongrel wagged its tail as I came up. Mercado regarded me with fearful eyes and yelled: "Go back, you fool. The dog is mad. It has rabies. Do you want to die?"

"Come down," I said. "It's not rabies. It's shaving cream. Look."

I patted the dog's head and whisked the foam away with my handkerchief. Mercado looked at me incredulously as I explained how he had been tricked. Panting and dishevelled he slid down the tree trunk.

"Dios," he said, reaching in his pocket for a bottle of iodine. He swabbed his scratches while I watched him disapprovingly.

"I don't know what you've been trying to do," I said. "But I am absolutely certain that you haven't done it."

He corked the vial and replaced it in his pocket. "Ah," he said, smiling brightly, "but I have."

I registered disbelief.

"Do you know what is in that small shed to the left of the house there?"

He pointed toward the ramshackle structure a few yards from the adobe house.

"No."

"The body of Juan Ruiz."

"What about it?"

"That is what we had to find. The body was necessary to them so we had to find it. I told Sammy that the body had been removed. I figured that would panic him into going to the place where the body was to check. That is why I had you follow him and Pedro."

"Even so, they've got away now."

Mercado shook his head. "Oh, no, they haven't. My plans are all working happily. You see, there is quite a little traffic on that little dirt road at dawn."

"Can you be less cryptic? I'm tired."

"Surely. At dawn that road is traveled by peons on their way to market. I stopped two of them and gave them messages to the *Jefe* of the next village. One took my message north, the other south."

"You mean that Sammy and Pedro will be stopped in the village by the *Jefe* there?"

"Of course. Now, let's us go along and see. I have instructed *el coronel* Gomez to meet us in Taxco this morning along with some other people."

"How did you get out here? In a car?"

"A taxi. I dismissed him and sent him back to town. I didn't expect to find you *inside* the house, you know."

I didn't discuss that point.

WE WENT back to our own car, turned it around and drove rapidly into the *pueblo* near the main road. We stopped in the middle of the village and a fat, swarthy man with a huge mustache came forward to greet us.

"I have him," he cried. "I have captured the great American gangster."

I grinned. I could well imagine what sort of message Mercado had sent in order to stir the local *Jefe* into action. Doubtless, it had contained chauvinistic references to the great republic of Mexico and its duty to apprehend the notorious gringo gangman who was about to perpetrate horrible depredations on homeland soil.

Mercado addressed a flowery sentence of praise to the *Jefe* who then led us to a mud and grass hut on the outskirts of the village. There, encased in gloom and tied securely to a post, sat Sammy and Pedro. The *Jefe* proudly produced the guns he had taken from them.

"Was there no trouble?" asked Mariano. "No difficulty in such a gallant capture?"

The *Jefe* beamed. "No, *señor*. I put my burro on the road to stop their car. Then five of us put machetes at their throats while we took their guns away."

"*Olé,*" said Mercado. "The Republic shall not forget."

The *Jefe* handed me the captured weapons. I held them on Sammy and Pedro as Mercado untied them. Then we herded them into the car. I sat with them in the back, keeping them covered. Mercado took his place at the wheel and headed into the lovely village of Taxco.

Thirty minutes later, I found myself in the office of the Ruiz mining company, situated just off Taxco's *zocalo*. In addition to Mercado and our prisoners, I discovered the presence of *el coronel* Gomez, a swarthy, beefy man, Drayton, Juan Ruiz' secretary and my compatriot, Apthorp.

As I herded Sammy and Pedro into chairs in a far corner of the room, I glanced inquiringly at Mercado. He smiled back at me.

"Señor Drayton is here because he was brought here by *el coronel* Gomez at my request. Señor Apthorp is here as a courtesy. I thought he would like to know what has happened."

Gomez cleared his throat and played with his mustache. "My little friend," he said to Mercado, "I am a busy man. I hope you have not forced me to travel all the way from Mexico City on some frivolous errand."

"Is murder frivolous?" asked Mercado rhetorically. "Is theft?"

Gomez shrugged. "Let us get down to cases."

"*Bueno.* First, Juan Ruiz is dead. He died a few days ago in Chapultepec Park. His body is in a shed some distance away."

"You mean," said Apthorp, "that he died *after* he signed my contract, of course. You know, I saw him that day."

"So did I," said Drayton emphatically.

"Neither of you did," said Mercado. "Apthorp *thought* he did. Drayton knew he didn't. Apthorp merely saw Pedro *twice.*"

"But," protested the American, "it couldn't be. They looked entirely different. They—"

Mercado held up a hand. "Wait," he said, "let me tell you exactly what happened. When the time came for the signing of that contract, Juan was dead. He would never have signed it while he was alive. But two signatures are necessary. So what happens? For some time Pedro has practised signing his brother's name. On the day the contract is ready, he has grown a mustache. He attires himself in decent clothes. He wears glasses and stands upright. He enters the room, signs and leaves. Moreover, he exchanges a few words of English with Apthorp."

There was silence in the room. Apthorp looked incredulous. Pedro and Sammy seemed scared. Drayton watched Mercado like a hawk.

"Then," went on Mercado, "Pedro leaves the room. He rushes into another room at the hotel—probably Drayton's—shaves his mustache off. Uses crepe hair and spirit gum on his face to give an unshaven tramp-like appearance, changes into dirty pants and shirt, puts on *huaraches,* then shambles back into Apthorp's presence. This time he can speak no English and he is not wearing glasses. His back is bent and he shuffles in pronounced contrast to his actions when he impersonated Juan.

"Moreover, he has another great advantage. Nationality is a funny thing. Americans say all Chinese look alike to them. To a Chinese all white men look almost alike, too. To Apthorp a Mexican is a Mexican. To him there isn't much different between them. Thus with Drayton helping the illusion out by addressing the first signer as Juan and the second as Pedro, he never dreams he is seeing the same man twice."

Gomez leaned forward and for the first time looked intensely interested.

"Go on," he said. "There must be more."

"There *is* more," said Mercado. "Pedro wanted money. But he is a crude operator. Twice he made attempts on his brother's life and failed. Drayton was aware of this. Then Drayton, in his role of trusted employee, heard that Apthorp was willing to pay a high price for the mine. Drayton knew quite well Juan would not sell, so he withheld the news of the offer and got in touch with Pedro, making a deal. But Drayton knew Pedro was a bungler so he imported an American gangman, Sammy, here, to do the actual killing.

"Drayton knew Juan had communicated with his friend Mendoza, that they had an appointment in the park that night. So it was easy for him to tip Sammy off when Juan left the hotel to keep the date with Mendoza. Sammy shot him in the head. The conspirators had a car ready to remove the corpse. But the car broke down. They were compelled to leave it there all night until the garages opened. So they hid the body in the bushes where the *tourista* found it—"

"I'm beginning to see it all now," I said. "Just at the time the car was fixed up, the tourist blundered on to Juan's body and ran howling down the path."

"Right," said Mercado. "That forced them to put the body in the car at once and in broad daylight. They couldn't wait for night as that would expose the fact that Juan never signed the sales contract. They were forced to gamble. Apparently, they did successfully. No one saw them put Juan in the car. But then a bright idea comes to them. Even if no body is found, the *tourista* will cause a police investigation. Perhaps Pedro has time to dab red paint on his head and take a pretended siesta in the bushes which will fix up everything. If they don't have time, they're just where they started but it's worth another gamble. It succeeded. Pedro is lying down with the paint on his head before anybody understands what the *tourista* is talking about."

"And Mendoza?" I said.

"Ah, Mendoza. Drayton was sure Mendoza suspected something, especially after he slugged Pedro. He was doubly worried after he knew Mendoza had called on me. Sammy called on him, thinking he knew or had figured much more than he did or had. Sammy killed him. Then came to threaten me, not being certain how much I knew.

"Now, they had to have Juan's body, in order to arrange for someone to find it a few weeks later to establish Juan is dead, and had been killed after he had signed the contract, so that Pedro could collect all the money. Without it, they'd have to wait for years until Juan would be declared legally dead before they could collect his share of the sale."

"So you told them the body had been taken in order to find out where it was?"

"Precisely."

DRAYTON SPOKE for the first time. "It's a nice theory. It's also entirely without proof."

"Sure," said Sammy, "you ain't got a thing on us, chum. If you don't leave me out of here the consul will hear of it."

Gomez turned a worried face to Mercado who smiled faintly.

"Sammy," he said, "you must know that there is no capital punishment in Mexico."

Sammy nodded. "Sure. Even if you had any evidence, which you ain't, I'd draw maybe a ten-year rap."

"Right," said Mercado. To Gomez he added: "Of course, there is the law of the fugitive. And Sammy here is a brave American gangman."

"Ah, yes," said Gomez, "the law of the fugitive."

"What cooks?" said Sammy Renault.

Mercado explained. "Our coppers are tough, Sammy. So, since there is no capital punishment in Mexico, it often happens that the perpetrators of heinous crimes try to escape. Naturally, it is the duty of the police to shoot them down."

"Naturally," said Gomez, "and a brave American gunman would not submit tamely to arrest. He would try to escape."

"Of course," said Mercado. "I am sure he will try to escape."

Sammy looked from one to the other apprehensively. "You mean—"

"We mean," said Mercado, "that if we get a complete confession involving your confederates, you will serve perhaps ten or fifteen years in prison. If you don't, then you will try to escape."

"And get killed," said Sammy with finality.

"It is very likely," said Mariano Mercado.

"I wouldn't have a chance," said Sammy.

"You wouldn't have a chance," said Mercado.

Sammy's face was suddenly nerveless. His facial muscles twitched. He could have done with a shot of heroin right then. He said tremulously: "Who do I talk to?"

"We shall go to the local *policia*," said Gomez, "all of us, and make arrangements there." He paused and eyed Mercado narrowly. "And the credit for arresting this American gunman?"

"Yours," said Mercado. "The last thought of a dying man was that I could help him. I've done so. The credit is yours, *mi coronel*."

Gomez stood up beaming. He advanced upon Mercado, flung his arms around him in Latin embrace. Their cheeks touched twice.

Mercado broke out of Gomez' grip with a shrill cry. His little hands patted his pockets then he turned to me with a face like death.

"*Dios!*" he cried like a wounded cat. "*Dios,* I forgot my atomizer. *Dios, Dios, Dios!*"

He ran like a madman from the room. From the window I saw him pounding pell mell over Taxco's ancient cobblestones in the general direction of the local *farmacia*.

SUITABLE FOR FRAMING

DOWN MEXICO WAY, MARIANO MERCADO SLYLY EVADED A GALAHAD CALL—AND SENT HIS ASSISTANT TO SAVE A LADY'S HONOR!

CHAPTER ONE
GERMLESS GENIUS

IT WAS almost dawn. There was a chill in the rarified Mexican air. A light tropical rain had been falling since eight o'clock in the evening. At four in the morning it had stopped. The streets gleamed wetly in the yellow light of the street lamps.

I sat, chain smoking, in the sterile apartment of Mariano Mercado. I was not comfortable. Mercado's chairs were not over-stuffed. As a matter of fact they were not stuffed at all.

It seemed that germs, bacteria and bacilli lived more contentedly in padded fabrics than on inhospitable wood and iron. Therefore Mercado's furniture was made of the latter materials. I was seated on a maple chair with a straight back and a bottom far more unyielding than mine. I had been sitting there for three and a half hours.

There was no urgency in my visit when I arrived but now I was beginning to become concerned. I had spent a plutocrat's evening, dining in Ciro's, dancing at El Patio and slumming in various unsavory *cantinas* in the company of a wide-eyed feminine *tourista* whom I had picked up in the American Express office.

At about one o'clock she thought I had insulted her, and I was positive that she had bored me, so we parted not too amicably. Not feeling sleepy and finding myself in the neighborhood of Mercado's sanitary lodgings, I had dropped in for a chat and a *habanero* before going to my hotel.

He had not answered my ring. However, in the role of employee, confidant and general confessor, I was possessed of a duplicate key. I let myself in, sat down uncomfortably and awaited his return.

I bent over, looked—and took a deep breath.

At three o'clock I began to wonder. Mercado was a man of temperate habits. While averse to neither a spot of alcoholic refreshment nor a touch of romance, he always managed to clean up both before midnight. It appeared that germ life flourished more potently in the darkness, that a man who retired early was a healthier one and that late hours weakened one's resistance, thus making the body a pushover for whatever parasite cared to attack it.

By now the sun had already climbed up from Vera Cruz and appeared over the rim of the plateau where Mexico City is situated. The bright light slanted through the Venetian blinds, making golden bars on the scrubbed wooden floor. And Mariano Mercado was still abroad. It was so unlike him that I resolved to give him until six o'clock, then telephone the accident wards of various hospitals.

Three minutes after I had made that decision, I heard light racing footfalls on the stairs. A key turned in the lock and Mariano Mercado burst into the room.

He was an ineffable sight. He had started out wearing a sword-creased green suit which had been cut by a daring and imaginative tailor. Now it hung like a robe of drenched burlap. His shirt, a natty two-tone job combining the worst features of puce and grey, was a sodden ruin. The colors of his tie—and I will swear there were thirteen

of them—had chummily run into each other. His shoes made a squishing sound as he walked and his hat was a wet blob of verdant felt.

This, in itself, was enough for the human eye to absorb before breakfast but there was more. The face of Mariano Mercado was a study in fear and horror. His eyes were rimmed with dark circles. His coffee-colored complexion had turned gray. Sheer panic was etched on his face.

I stood up and put out my cigarette. I said: "What on earth's the matter?"

Mariano Mercado did not answer me. He turned his face toward the ceiling and addressed a personage of greater influence. "*Valgame Dios,*" he murmured. That, in Spanish, is usually an oath. It was not this time—it was a prayer.

Then he turned his wild-eyed gaze on me and went into action. "The bath, Latham. And *pronto.* As hot as you can get it."

Even as he spoke he began to rip off his clothes like a strip tease artist who wants to get home early. I went into the bathroom, turned on the hot water and returned. By this time Mercado stood stark naked before his desk.

His trembling brown hand was poised over an array of bottles on the blotter. Hastily he selected three of them. He filled a glass with triple-distilled water and gulped down one pill from each bottle.

"Calomel, aspirin and quinine," he said. "They may save me."

He dashed past me like a marathon runner, raced into the bathroom and plunged into the tub like a man whose clothes were on fire. I followed him in, sat on the edge of the basin and said for the second time: "What's the matter?"

"Nada," he said with the brave tremulous smile of a Christian martyr, "nothing at all, except that I shall probably die."

This did not alarm me. Mariano Mercado died several times a week. If he saw a fly approaching at a hundred yards he was certain it was either tsetse or malarial. Every dish from which he ate was the host for a googol of germs.

I said quite calmly: "And what shall you die of this time?"

He soaped his brown chest "Pneumonia, tuberculosis, bronchitis or pleurisy. Evilio Torga has murdered me."

NOW EVILIO Torga was the proprietor of a *cantina* often frequented by Mercado and myself. He was a huge fat man, jovial and fond of a joke. He was free handed and pleasant. It was impossible to conceive of Evilio Torga murdering anyone at all and I said as much.

"He is a villain of the deepest dye," said Mercado. "He has sent me to my grave. He—"

At this point he sneezed. An expression of terror spread over his face. He said sepulchrally: "Mercado is not long for this world."

"Mercado," I said, "will outlive the sphinx. You're as healthy as a bottle of tonic. But tell me what horrible thing Torga did."

"Listen," said Mariano Mercado gravely, "Listen to the tale of an assassin."

It appeared that, about ten o'clock, Mercado had been drinking *habanero* in Torga's saloon. It had begun to rain. Torga's telephone was out of commission and Mercado had been unable to call a taxi.

Now, Mercado would no more have thought of going out in a storm sans raincoat, rubbers, bumbershoot and muffler, than he would have considered tossing a bomb into the chambers of *el President* Aleman. So, quite naturally, he remained where he was.

It kept on raining and Mercado kept on leaning against the bar sipping drinks. At three-thirty he was the only customer and Evilio Torga manifested an understandable desire to go home.

In Mexico City there is no closing law. The custom of the country is for the saloon keeper to keep his doors ajar until the clients have departed, then run down his iron shutters.

Torga politely invited Mercado to leave, Mercado peered outside at the rain and flatly refused. An argument ensued, whereupon Torga stood on his proprietory rights and ordered poor Mercado out onto the street.

Mercado had eventually gone, with all the enthusiasm of a man walking to the electric chair. At this hour the taxis were gone from the streets and Mercado had walked home in the wet, covering a distance of almost two miles.

On several occasions he had taken refuge in friendly doorways and the journey had taken him some time. Drenched to the skin, he was thoroughly convinced that he was a dead man. And he was unshakable in his conviction that Evilio Torga had murdered him.

He concluded his tale and looked at me reproachfully when he found me unsympathetic. He got out of the tub, rubbed himself vigorously and searched the medicine closet for more remedies. In that well-stocked chest he found several.

He was pouring a sticky dark mixture down his gullet when the telephone rang. I wandered out of the steaming bathroom and answered it.

A voice, obviously mid-west United States, said in execrable Spanish: *"Esta abierto la officina?"*

I said, in English: "Are you asking if the office is open?"

"Yeah. That's right. Are you open for business yet? If not, what time *do* you open?"

Even in English it was a difficult question. Mercado had no office hours. It was strictly forbidden to disturb him during the siesta hours, but beyond that the office was open whenever either of us was in it.

I wasn't sleepy and I knew Mercado was far too concerned over his imminent demise to rest. I said: "If it's important, you can come over now."

The voice thanked me fervently and, without giving me a name, cut off.

I found Mercado in the bedroom. He had a red woolen muffler about his neck and his little body was wrapped in a heavy bathrobe. Some of the panic had gone from his expression, had been replaced by a look of mild incredulity, as if he were surprised to find that he was still alive.

"Was that Torga on the phone? Overcome by remorse, perhaps?"

"It was not Torga. It was a client, I gather."

"Send him away. I am in no condition for work."

"You'd better be," I told him. "Our combined bank balances total something under five hundred pesos. You'd better do whatever this gringo wants and for whatever you can get."

"What does he want?"

"I haven't the faintest idea. He sounded like a country-man of mine in some trouble."

"I didn't know your countrymen got up so early."

It was useless to tell him that the American *tourista* is not typical of the average citizen. Mercado considered that all Americans were fat, well heeled, arrogant and lazy. Judging from the caliber of the *touristas* who infested Mexico, I cannot say that I found it in my heart to blame him.

It was a little before seven o'clock when the doorbell pealed. By this time Mercado was sitting at his desk dosing himself periodically with the contents of various bottles and vials. I got up from my uncomfortable chair and went to answer the door.

THE MAN upon the threshold was a perfect example of Mercado's conception of an American. He was of middle age. He was fat. He apparently had money and his manner was brusque and condescending. He said: "I'm Thomas Lapley. Where's Mercado?"

I nodded and led him into the office. As we came into the Mercadian presence, I said: "The *señor* Mercado is somewhat indisposed. Perhaps he will not be able to help you today."

Lapley laughed a Chamber of Commerce laugh. He said with profound conviction: "He'll help me, all right. I'm quite willing to be overcharged."

He extracted a thick wallet from his pocket, plunged two pudgy fingers into it and withdrew an enormous mass of Mexican bills. He flung them on the desk and said: "There's three thousand pesos. What do you say to that, Mr. Mercado?"

Mr. Mercado said nothing to that. As a matter of fact, he shrank back in his chair, registered anguish and said in a weak voice: "Latham, take that away."

Thomas Lapley, who doubtless had never seen a man flinch in the face of three thousand pesos in his life, looked astonished. But this was a familiar situation to me.

I scooped the bills up from the desk and put them in my pocket. Mercado grabbed a large bottle of disinfectant, spilled some on the desk where the money had lain and scrubbed vigorously with his handkerchief.

"For the love of Pete," said Mr. Lapley, "what's wrong?"

Mariano Mercado paused in his labors. He fixed Lapley with a reproachful eye. He said: "Do you have any idea of how many germs there are on a single peso note?"

Mr. Lapley blinked. It was obvious that he had not the slightest idea of how many germs there were on a single peso note. But I knew to the last decimal point. I had heard it often enough. Morever, I had no desire at all to hear it again.

I said hastily: "Since Mr. Lapley has seen fit to call on us so early in the morning, his business is undoubtedly important. Suppose we listen to what he has to say."

I drew up a chair and Lapley deposited his bulk in it. He said very seriously: "It is important. Also pretty incredible. That is why I am prepared to pay such a high price for some help."

Mariano Mercado opened his mouth, thrust the nozzle of an atomizer in it and sprayed away. He set the bottle down on the desk again and said: "All right, what is it?"

"Well," said Lapley, "it is a matter of honor."

Mercado blinked. He did not associate American businessmen with honor.

"A lady's honor," said Lapley solemnly and Mercado blinked again.

"I had a letter in my possession," went on Lapley. "An indiscreet letter written by a lady. If the contents of this missive were to come to light the results would be disastrous for this woman."

Mercado nodded. "And you have lost the letter?"

"In a sense. Only in a sense. A few hours ago I was alone in my hotel room. I had the letter in my possession. I also had an automatic pistol I had just bought."

"Why did you buy the pistol?" asked Mercado.

"For protection. I was afraid that some unscrupulous people would want to take the letter from me by force. And I was right. I was just about to load the gun when I heard the outer door of my suite open. Instinct told me that it was the man who wanted that letter. My gun was still unloaded. What could I do?"

The question was rhetorical and required no answer. Thomas Lapley continued.

"The letter was in my pocket. Hastily I rolled it up and jammed it in the magazine of my gun. No sooner had I done that than this other person entered the room with a thirty-eight in his hand."

Mercado's expression was frankly sceptical. Lapley, however, did not seem to notice it.

"He disarmed me at gun point, tied me up and searched the premises. Naturally, he did not think of looking in the magazine of my automatic. He found nothing of interest.

"Then my telephone rang. I told him that the front desk knew I was in and if I didn't answer the phone they'd come up to investigate. That scared him and he left. I left the hotel shortly afterwards. In my excitement I forgot my gun which is still lying on the table in the bedroom."

"This," said Mariano Mercado, "is a most interesting story. What do you want me to do?"

"I want you to go to my hotel—suite 398, La Paloma—and retrieve that gun and the letter it contains."

"Why can't you go yourself, thus saving a great number of pesos?"

Lapley shook his head. "Because I am afraid my adversary may be waiting for me outside the hotel. He might kidnap and torture me to reveal the hiding place of the letter."

Mercado swallowed a pill thoughtfully. "And to what address shall I return the automatic?"

Lapley took a card from his pocket and scribbled something on it. "There," he said, "I shall wait for you there. Will you go for the gun immediately?"

There was a long pause. I turned Lapley's story over in my mind and decided it sounded as phony as the clink of a lead half dollar. Mercado nodded suddenly and said: "*Señor,* we accept your commission." Lapley wrung his hand fervently, then shook mine and headed for the door uttering profuse thank-yous.

WHEN HE had gone, I found Mariano Mercado regarding me calculatingly.

"Latham," he said, "can you be objective?"

"To a degree."

"Very well. I want you to consider a hypothetical question."

I lit a cigarette and sat down. "Shoot."

"From a purely objective point of view, which, in your opinion would be the better all-around situation: For me to languish in jail while you used your brains and influence to get me out, or for you to be in jail while I exercised mine?"

I thought it over with some apprehension. "Personally," I said, "I would far prefer to see you in jail. However, honesty and objectivity compel me to admit that you possess quicker wits and more influence than I do. I am sure you'd get me out quicker than I could get you. But why?"

"I am salving my conscience," said Mercado.

"Has this anything to do with Lapley?"

"It has everything to do with Lapley. One more question: You have no qualms about sharing Lapley's fee with me?"

"Of course not. Haven't we an agreement that I'm to collect forty percent of all fees?"

"We have. My conscience is almost clear. Another thing: you have no fear of bacteria?"

"Well," I said, "I wouldn't drink from a typhus infested well, but beyond that I can face bacterial peril without panic."

"My conscience is lulled to sleep," said Mercado. "Get your hat on."

"For what?"

"You are going to the La Paloma hotel. Suite three ninety-eight. To retrieve Lapley's gun."

"You really believe his story? You believe the gun is there?"

"I believe the gun is there. Go and get it."

I stood up, shrugged and reached for my hat. I didn't know what Lapley's angle was but I was certain that there was no truth whatever in his tale. Mercado reached for his atomizer and I went down the hall to the door.

It was after eight o'clock when I got into the street. The careening buses were jammed with people going to work. The street cars jangled perilously around corners with humanity hanging on by teeth and fingernails.

I saw a *libre* coming down the street and hailed it. Twenty minutes later I paid the taxicab at the entrance to the La Paloma and entered the lobby.

It occurred to me as I mounted the stairs that I had no key to the room. I decided to try the door on the off-chance that it might be open and, if that failed, to tell some wild tale to the clerk in order to obtain access.

However, luck was with me. Or so I thought at the time.

The door was unlocked. The knob turned easily in my hand and I entered the overfurnished living room of the hotel suite. The chamber, vast and musty, was empty. I strode through it toward a door which apparently gave on to the bedroom. I threw this open and went in.

Since I had hardly believed a word of Lapley's weird tale, I was mildly surprised to observe that one major item of it checked. There *was* an automatic on the table near the bed.

I picked it up and dropped it in my pocket, reflecting that this was the easiest batch of pesos that either Mariano Mercado or I had earned in many a long *dia*.

I was about to leave the room with a sense of task easily and well done when I saw the shoes under the bed. I stared at them and my stomach slowly turned over.

The shoes were not empty, neither were they laid flat on the floor. The toes were pointed toward the carpet on which they rested, and the heels were aimed at the ceiling. It needed no quick wit to realize that there was a man under the bed lying on his face.

I bent over and looked. I saw a short, rather paunchy figure, lying very still. I took a deep breath, straightened up again and pulled the bed to one side.

A second examination showed me the two red holes in the back of the man's coat. He had been shot in the back and in the heart. As a matter of routine I reached for his pulse. I found out only what I already knew. He was dead.

I reached in my pocket for a cigarette, lighted it and sat on the edge of the bed. Half a dozen theories sprang to my mind, none of them full blown.

Mercado was infinitely better at this sort of thing than I was. I decided to leave the corpse where it was, phone Mercado from a booth in the lobby and acquaint him with the facts. He could make up his mind whether he wanted to pocket the fee and lay the corpse in the lap of the *policia* or handle it himself.

It occurred to me that perhaps knowledge of the corpse's identity would be useful. I put my cigarette out and bent over the dead man. I rolled him over on his back and proceeded to go through his pockets.

My macabre task was interrupted by a guttural and too familiar voice saying: *"Madre de Dios!* I have you red-handed. And where is that other murderer, Mercado?"

There was a sudden vacuum at the pit of my stomach and half a dozen ice cubes seemed to touch the end of my spine. I removed my hand from the dead man's breast pocket and turned my head around to see *el coronel* Gomez of the *Departmento de Policia.*

CHAPTER TWO
THE TUMBRILS ROLL

GOMEZ WAS a stout, swarthy man with a pair of elegant mustachios of which he was inordinately proud. He was possessed of infinite conceit, unlimited arrogance and an intense dislike of Mariano Mercado which was broad enough to include me.

I said, rather foolishly: "I can explain this."

Gomez took a huge piece of ordnance from his pocket, covered me and ran his free hand through my coat. He removed Lapley's automatic, holding it carefully by the muzzle.

He said: "A dead man and a gun in your pocket. Probably with fingerprints on it. If the ballistics department confirms what I believe to be true, I do not think any explanation you make will be satisfactory, Señor Latham."

Now, I am no genius. I am not the most quick-witted man in all the world. But I knew, beyond all doubt, that I had been framed. What exactly had been Thomas Lapley's object I did not know. But at the moment I was the fall guy.

I knew it was idiotic to tell Lapley's tale to Gomez. If Lapley's story was so wild that I hadn't accepted it, it was a cinch that Gomez wasn't going to believe me.

I said: "*Coronel,* I want to see Mercado."

He grinned. "We have that desire in common. I was hoping to find him here. But I see he sends his assistant to perform his bloody work."

I blinked at that. "You mean you think Mercado and I killed this *hombre?*"

Gomez bowed courteously. "I merely make the arrests," he said. "The prosecutor will discuss the matter with you."

"You mean I'm pinched? You're going to take me to the police station?"

El coronel Gomez nudged me in the back with his oversized revolver. "I am not taking you to the bullfight," he said. "Let us proceed. *Vamanos!*"

Less than an hour later I was developing Mercado's attitude toward germ life. A Mexican prison is no white-tiled sanctuary. It is neither modern, sanitary, nor beneficent.

My cell was dark and windowless. On the floor lay a pallet which had been used at least once before. Fleas danced gayly in the straw. There was no lavatory, and the food which had been brought me consisted of a dirty tin plate covered with greasy beans, a cup of brackish water and a tortilla at least four days old.

When Gomez had locked me in he had politely promised to get in immediate touch with Mariano Mercado. However, lunchtime was far behind me and no one had yet appeared.

At four o'clock I was hungry, angry and, to be candid about it, afraid. After all, Gomez had nailed me in a hotel suite with a corpse and a gun—a gun which doubtless bore my fingerprints. All I had on my side was an utterly incredible story about Lapley and a woman's honor. By this time I was certain that there was no incriminating letter in the automatic's magazine. I was painfully certain that there were bullets there instead, eight of them anyway. The other two were in the dead man's back.

At four-thirty I heard heavy footfalls on the concrete of the passageway outside my cell, and a few seconds later the bulk of *el coronel* Gomez hove into view. He fitted a key into my cell door. I noted that he was scowling.

"That *cabrone*, Mercado," he said. And added three unprintable Spanish oaths. "He knows the *politicos*. He has used his influence to have you released upon his recognizance. But remember you are not free. As soon as I have the report from the ballistics people I will have enough evidence to take you despite Mercado and his petty officials. You are to go to Mercado immediately and remain in his sight all the time."

I didn't pause for conversation. I flicked some fleas from my lapel and headed out for the street on the double. I hailed the first taxi I saw and rode through the streets to Mercado's apartment.

HE HAD recovered somewhat from his morning's alarm. He had discarded his bathrobe and donned a suit of bright brown which looked rather like an inferior brand of milk chocolate. His shirt was Erin's flag, and his tie motley.

He was cautiously squeezing yellow beads from a medicine dropper into a glass of water as I entered. He looked up, saw me, and said gravely: *"Dios,* it was worse than I expected."

"It was a damned sight worse than *I* expected," I said. "What the devil—"

I broke off as he looked at me in horror.

"Dios, Latham," he said. "Get away from my desk. Get away. Stand over in the far corner of the room."

His voice had risen and the final syllable was a falsetto scream.

"For Heaven's sake," I said, shaken by this reception, "what's the matter with you? You don't think I'm a murderer, too, do you?"

"Murderer?" he said. "No. But you're infested. You've been in a cell. You're alive with fleas, with bacteria. You could kill a regiment as you stand. Keep away from me."

He had snatched up a Flit gun which always laid on the top of his desk and furiously assaulted the invisible hosts in the air.

I retreated to a far corner of the room. Mercado put down the Flit gun and reached for an atomizer. As he sprayed his throat I recalled something he had said early that morning.

"Listen," I said, "You were talking about salving your conscience this morning. Did you know I was going to jail?"

"I suspected it."

"And you let me go anyway?"

"I wanted to see what Señor Lapley was up to."

"Well, you certainly found out," I said bitterly. "Do you realize I'm facing a murder rap? Do you realize that they have one hell of a lovely case against me?

He nodded and sighed. "It was very well thought out, wasn't it?"

"Damn it. Do you have to be so impersonal about it? Do you want me to hang?"

"There is no capital punishment in Mexico," he said reassuringly. "You forget we are a civilized country."

That was comforting as hell and I said so. I added: "Did you really have any idea what Lapley was up to?"

"Of course. His story, as even you noticed, was idiotic. No one would have believed it. No one was intended to but us. Lapley thought that all those pesos he threw on the desk would blind our judgment."

"But it didn't?" I said with a withering sarcasm which was utterly wasted on Mercado.

"It did not," he said. "I knew what he was up to. He wanted to stick us with such a weird story that when we told it to the police they would not believe it."

"But you didn't know there was a murder involved?"

"I suspected it."

"How?"

"That yarn about the letter in the automatic. And the fact that he wanted me to go and get the gun. It was apparent that he wanted me to pick the weapon up. That would plant my fingerprints on it and help tighten the case against me."

"Against *you?*" I said indignantly. "You mean against me."

"That is of no moment. Lapley expected me to go to the hotel. I sent you instead."

"My Lord," I said. "I have half a mind to buy myself some leprosy germs and drop them in your coffee. You had a good idea what was going on and *you sent me instead.* Why the devil didn't you go yourself? It was you he was hiring."

"I was afraid," said Mariano Mercado with devastating simplicity.

I stared at him. I had seen Mercado tackle a thug armed with a knife and overpower him with his bare brown hands. I had seen him gaze blandly into the muzzle of a gun and spit Spanish insult.

I said: "Afraid? Of what?"

"Of exactly what happened. I was afraid that someone would get arrested. If arrested he would be thrown in a cell. I would rather face a battalion of wild elephants than spend an hour in a Mexican prison."

I got it then. Mercado had sent me, anticipating the frame and realizing it was quite likely that whoever entered the hotel room would eventually be pinched. And Mariano Mercado certainly did not possess the courage to cope with the fleas, lice and invisible parasites which infested the jail.

But the fact of my understanding his actions did in no wise mitigate my own circumstances. Unless something speedy and drastic was done I would face a trial for murder with no better than a fifty percent chance of beating the rap.

I mentioned this none too calmly and added: "So what do we do first?"

"Find Lapley."

I laughed without mirth. "There are twenty million people in Mexico, the area is seven hundred and sixty thousand odd square miles. How are we going to do it? *Cantina* by *cantina* or *pueblo* by *pueblo?*"

"It is simpler than that," said Mercado. "First, there is little doubt that this Lapley, as he calls himself, is an American."

"So what?"

"If he is an American he possesses either a passport or a tourist card."

That, of course, made it easier. Then a depressing thought occurred to me. "But how do we find him? Thomas Lapley certainly is a phony name."

Mercado nodded. "The name is phony. But the initials aren't. He wore a signet ring marked with the letters *T.L.*

He was intelligent enough to use a false name which began with those initials."

Now I felt better than I had since early morning. "So I go to the passport office and look for an American whose initials are T.L. If that fails I check the tourists cards. And if I find Lapley do you think you can pin that killing on him?"

Mercado shook his head. His bland air of unconcern nettled me.

"Well, why not?" I demanded.

"Because," said Mercado, "I don't think this Lapley committed any murder."

"Then who did?"

Mercado sighed, spread his palms upward and achieved a magnificent shrug of his thin shoulders.

"You go and check up on Lapley," he said. "In the meantime, I'll find out what I can about the murdered man. And you'd better hurry."

I threw him a savage glance. After all, *I* was the guy who was in trouble. I needed no gratuitous advice as to speed.

AT THE passport office I had no luck at all. There were no foreign characters who bore the initials *T.L.* However, in the office which keeps an official eye on *touristas,* I had a little more luck than I expected.

Not only did I find an American whose description answered that of Thomas Lapley but his name, it seemed, was Theodore Lamb. In addition to this break, the recorded dates showed that his tourist card expired in three more days.

Now a Mexican tourist card which is granted to Americans in lieu of a passport is good for six months. After that period has expired it must be renewed for a second six months. Morever it must be renewed on the precise day it becomes invalid. Otherwise the luckless tourist will find himself spending the night on a straw pallet similar to the one that I had just deserted.

I telephoned Mercado and reported all this. He acknowledged the news and said: "Well, then, hang around. When this Lapley or Lamb shows up, follow him and find out where he lives. We're going to need him."

I said: "All right. And what about you? Have you masterminded anything?"

His voice, as he replied, did not exactly surge with hope. "I am pursuing certain lines of investigation," he said primly. "Be patient and do not worry. Rest assured that if there should be a miscarriage of justice here, I shall avenge you."

That, of course, was just jolly. I could spend ten odd years sleeping on straw, dining on frijoles and goat meat, all the while solacing myself that Mercado would see to it that I was avenged.

Espying a *cantina* across the street from the tourist bureau, I went over there and ordered a stiff and straight shot of tequila. I drank it quickly, then took an encore. I took several encores, after which I slowed down a bit. After all, I had two days to kill.

The tourist office was open from ten in the morning until four in the afternoon. I made those my hours, too. It was an arduous job. After all, one cannot sit in a *cantina* staring blankly at the transparent glass which encloses the men's room. It looks odd. One must drink.

I had consumed, at a rough estimate, four and a half litres of tequila when I caught sight of Lapley's pompous figure entering the tourist office. Aware of the fact that Mexican officialdom does not function at breakneck speed, I decided I had time for a large cup of *café negro* to sober me up a little.

I ordered it and drank it before Lapley emerged from the office. He blinked in the brilliant sunlight, waddled to the corner and hailed a *libre*. I went along after him and hailed the next one.

It was a full hour before lunch time and the traffic was not dense. Both our cabs went along leisurely toward the west side of town. The closely built houses of the city finally became sparser as we gained the suburbs. The cab in front of me turned off into a dirt road. I instructed my driver to follow, promised him extra pesos, and counseled him that discretion was of the essence.

We moved along a winding dirt road, climbing a mountain in the process. We crossed a rickety wooden bridge flung across the turbulent stream which poured hissingly over the rocks. Then in the distance I descried a pair of stone columns which indicated the presence of an elaborate house. I was a good half mile behind when I saw my quarry stop.

I halted my own cab.

"Wait here," I said. "Drive back to that last turnoff and wait for me there. I don't know how long I'll be but I'll see you have a profit."

My driver flashed a set of glamorous teeth at me and did as I bade him. I set off on foot toward the distant stone columns.

As I approached I saw that the columns were part of a magnificent hacienda. It stood proudly against a blue sky, and in the midst of a luxurious tropical garden. About a hundred yards on this side of it stood a fenced-in modest bungalow. As I neared it I saw two children playing on the verandah.

The bungalow was neat and trim, the garden well cared for, and the children clean and charming. Yet, somehow, with the background of the château-like building next door, I received a strong impression that the occupants of the smaller structure were not well-to-do.

I waited around for some time. At the end of an hour Lamb emerged from the big house and climbed back into his taxi. I concealed myself behind a huge Indian Laurel tree and when he had passed made a wild dash on foot for my own *libre*.

I made it in time to pick up his trail and follow him back to town.

There, Lamb's taxi drew up before the Ritz hotel where he paid off and dismissed his driver. I followed suit, waiting a few moments, then went into the lobby.

I approached the desk, pressed ten pesos on the clerk, and possessed myself of the information that *el señor* Lamb was a resident of the hotel and had been for some six months.

I had one more tequila in the Ritz bar and took myself off to Mercado's. I had done my job. I was hoping to high heaven that he had done something, too.

WHEN I arrived he was immersed in a medical journal. He said: "Latham, how far can a mosquito fly?"

"I made Phi Beta without knowing that," I said. "I guess I can get along without the knowledge. Why?"

"I am reading of the Virgin Islands. It seems elephantiasis is prevalent there. It is caused by the bite of a mosquito which prowls at night. Do you think a mosquito could fly fifteen hundred odd miles?"

I stared at him, a slow anger arising within me. I said: "*Hijo de perra*, I am walking about with a ten year sentence for murder hanging over my head. Instead of concerning yourself with me you are worrying that some damned supermosquito is going to fly from the Virgin Islands and bite you. *Dios!* What have you done regarding *me?*"

He waved a brown and deprecatory hand. "Do not excite yourself," he said. "It raises blood pressure and hardens arteries. I have made my investigations. But what about you?"

I gave him a full report of my activities, and asked again of his.

He said again: "I have investigated."

"With what result?"

"The murdered man was Luis Ortega. He has had something of a checkered career. He was of good family and sowed a bumper crop of wild oats in his youth. He once spent some time in prison. He dissipated his patrimony and—"

"Will you get to the point? I am not at all interested in the drunken amours of *Señor Ortega.*"

"Very well. A few years ago he entered the export business and made a lot of money. However speculation in silver lost most of it for him and his business was in danger. He needed capital and needed it quickly. When he was murdered he was on the verge of ruin."

Mercado stopped with an air of finality and helped himself liberally to cod liver oil.

I said: "Well, go on."

"Go on? That is all."

"Well," I said bitterly, "I am glad I am going to jail with full knowledge of the affairs of Mr. Ortega. It would have been quite unbearable to spend my life in a cell unaware of the Ortega business affairs." I dropped my forced calm and shouted angrily: "What good does all this irrelevant information do me?"

Mercado lifted his eyebrows. "Perhaps it did none a few minutes ago. But in the light of the information you obtained it might conceivably help you a great deal."

"What valuable information did I bring in? Save, perhaps, Lamb's address?"

"You discovered that Lamb knows Grannick. There may be a connection there."

"Why? Who's Grannick?"

Mercado sighed and his face assumed the doleful expression common to it when he spoke of physical infirmities.

"He is an old man," he said. "An old man with a heart weak as American coffee. However, he is a tough old man, though hardly as tough as his uncle. That was his house you saw today."

I settled back in my chair and resigned myself to hearing some more family history. Mercado knew everyone in Mexico City. Moreover, he knew their genealogy.

"His uncle, dead some twenty-five years, was an American who became a naturalized Mexican citizen. He was appalled at the lawlessness of this country some forty years back and set out to do what he could to rectify it. He entered politics and eventually became a Federal judge."

"Must you gossip," I said, "while I hear the tumbrils roll?"

Mercado ignored me. "Old man Grannick, the uncle, had a phobia against crime and criminals. He considered all law breakers equal—the pickpocket was no less guilty than the murderer."

"I get it," I said sarcastically. "I'm supposed to be grateful that I can't come before him for sentence."

Mercado picked up the cod liver pills, put them down and had halibut liver instead.

"He left a son," he went on blandly. "And a nephew and one hell of a lot of money. He cut the son out of his will because as a youth he served six months for assault—some sort of a tavern brawl. The son is now dead although I believe he had issue. Grannick, the nephew, has not."

"Goody," I said without enthusiasm. "And will you write me long letters about the rest of it while I'm serving my time? I understand prisoners just love to get mail."

Again he ignored me. He stood up and took from the clothes tree a hat whose green would have caused a leaf to tremble. He put it upon his head, adjusted a tie which would have penetrated to the iris of a blind man, and said: *"Estas listo?"*

"Sure, I'm ready. Where are we going?"

"Out to Grannick's. I'd rather like a look around. This afternoon I must do some work which may save you from this prison you're always harping about."

I checked the angry answer which rose to my lips. If a guy isn't entitled to harp about ten years of penal servitude, I'd like to know what he *is* allowed to gripe about.

I reached for my own hat and followed Mercado into the sunshine of the street. There we hailed a taxi and set out for the Grannick place.

WE RODE through the suburbs retracing the route I had followed earlier. We crossed the rickety bridge from which we could see the stone columns of Grannick's place. We were at least a half mile away when Mercado cried, *"Pare!"* and got out of the cab.

He told the man to wait, and set off on foot. I followed him, puzzled.

"Why the walk?" I asked.

"I desire to think," said Mariano Mercado. "I find I do so more effectively without the stink of gasoline fumes in my nostrils."

I let it go at that and plodded along behind him.

In a few minutes we reached the flower-covered cottage which stood just to the west of the Grannick place. The front gate was open and the two children I had seen before were playing in the yard. As we approached, the boy was staring at a small pool of water in the ground before him.

He said in his high voice: "Let us make mud pies."

His sister frowned. "No," she said emphatically. "It's dirty. You get germs all over you."

"What's germs?" said the boy.

Mercado stopped dead and shamelessly eavesdropped this conversation.

"Germs," said the girl, and her solemn mien while discussing this subject reminded me of a juvenile Mercado, "are nasty things. They give you diseases. You can't see them but they're there and they're more dangerous than lions, even than elephants."

"*Olé,*" cried Mercado. "A precocious child."

The children turned grave faces toward him. He fumbled in his pocket and produced two *tostones.*

He proffered them to the children. The boy glanced uncertainly at his sister who shook her head emphatically.

"*Gracias, no,*" she said.

Mercado lifted his eyebrows. "And why not?"

"We must not take money from strangers. Besides money is dirty. It has germs all over it."

Mercado stood entranced. He beamed happily like a missionary who has just saved a soul.

"What a wonderful *niños*," he exclaimed. "And what are your names?"

"I'm Juanita Grannick," said the girl. "My brother is Juan."

Mercado looked at me significantly. "Old man Grannick's grandchildren," he murmured. More loudly, he said: "And that is the house of your uncle over there?"

He pointed to the *hacienda*. The girl nodded. "But," she said gravely, "we never see him. He is rich. We are poor. Our *madre* has to work."

Mercado patted her on the head. He seemed suddenly abstracted. He said, *"Adios,* little ones," and walked away. I followed him.

As we got back to the car, I said: "Well, where are we now?"

Mercado scratched his head thoughtfully. "I'm not quite sure. But it occurs to me that if old man Grannick cut off his son because of a minor peccadillo, he certainly would do the same thing to his nephew."

"And what does that mean?"

"You'll recall I told you this Ortega who was killed had a prison record."

I said again: "What does *that* mean?"

"I'm not quite sure but I'll go to work tomorrow morning. I'll probably have a definite answer for you then."

CHAPTER THREE
FREE MAN OR FELON?

I SLEPT on that but not restfully. I was up at dawn. I ate breakfast and went to Mercado's apartment, but he had already gone. I put in a long nervous day. Mercado came home a little after six o'clock.

He refused to talk to me until he had performed his disinfecting rites and swallowed his vitamins and other mysterious nostrums. Then he carefully dusted off the seat of his chair and put himself into it.

He said: "I have spent the day in the Probate Court studying the Grannick will. It is much as I thought it would be."

"Does it keep me out of jail?"

"Perhaps," he said and I failed to note a lot of conviction in his tone. "We shall see in a little while. I have communicated with Gomez instructing him to pick up this Lamb and conduct him out to Grannick's mansion. We, too, are due there right away. *Vamanos!*"

After that he shut up like a taciturn clam and my questions elicited no answer at all.

It was about seven o'clock in the evening when we set out for Grannick's mansion. A mantle of dark, menacing clouds hung in the sky. The air held a sultriness not often felt at this altitude.

We had taken Mercado's ancient coupé out of the garage where it was pasturing, to make the trip. We rattled across the rickety bridge in the last light of day.

I was driving, and frowning at the road. Mercado had been most secretive about his researches and I considered myself an interested party. I slowed down, lighted a *Delicado,* and said: "Well, how do I stand now? Am I a felon or a free man?"

Mariano Mercado pulled a sigh up from his boot straps and let it go like a melancholy wind. He said: "With luck, you're a free man. What is your opinion of this Lamb?"

"I'm glad you asked me," I said bitterly. "I am the one man in Mexico qualified to give an expert opinion. Señor Lamb is a—"

I ran out of unprintable epithets in three minutes. Then Mercado said mildly: "I did not mean that. Do you think he is a man of stamina or will he crack under pressure?"

"He's fat and soft. He'll probably crack. Why?"

Mercado sighed again. "As I have things worked out, your fate probably depends on him. I can explain everything but I'm going to need some tangible evidence. I am hoping to get it from Lamb."

My stomach was filled with an apprehensive emptiness. I glared at him. "Do I understand that my fate depends on your obtaining a confession of murder from Lamb?"

"Not exactly a confession of murder, but a confession, *sí.*"

I said: "Will you bring me cigarettes on visitors' day?" Then I laughed wildly and without mirth. Mercado regarded me gravely but he did not speak. We made the rest of the journey in silence.

As we passed the modest home of the Grannick grandchildren I noted a uniformed man on the verandah engaged in tacking up a poster on the wall. I wondered for a moment if the working widow had defaulted on the mortgage and was about to be dispossessed in the best tradition, then I dismissed it from my mind. My personal problems were too pressing.

A moment later we disembarked at the rambling stone mansion of Ricardo Grannick. We were the last arrivals. A servant admitted us, led us into a vast living room with a stone fireplace and luxurious leather chairs. *El coronel* Gomez leaned against the mantelpiece smoking a cigar and twirling his mustachios.

Across the room Grannick, a blanket around his shoulders, sat slumped in a chair which was far too big for him. He looked like an old man. His eyes were sunken deeply in his head, his face was wrinkled and the color of old leather.

Half ensconced behind the curtain on the window seat was Lamb. It seemed to me that some of his pomposity was gone. His round face was grave and there was an expression of anxiety in his eyes.

The introductions were performed and a servant produced a bottle of *aguadiente* and some glasses. Grannick abstained but the rest of us drank, and I thought with relish.

Gomez set his glass down with a clinking sound and said abruptly: "Well, little man, and why have you called this meeting?"

"You already have the corpse," said Mercado. "I have come to give you the killer."

THESE WERE brave words. But considering what he had said to me in the car I took little heart from them. I still had a picture of myself wallowing in a vermin-infested cell for the rest of my life.

Everyone glanced toward Mercado. He seemed assured and if he didn't know what he was doing he certainly gave the impression that he did.

Gomez opened his mouth to speak again but before he could do so the storm broke. A sheet of rain belted down on the roof and the wind raced over the plain, bending the trees before it. Lightning flashed in the sky and thunder crashed like artillery off to the left.

Gomez lifted his voice. He said: "I have the killer. I have Latham."

Mercado shook his head and I lit another cigarette with fingers which in no wise resembled the Rock of Gibraltar.

"Latham is not your man," said Mercado.

Gomez shrugged and spread his palms. "I am not a court. Let them decide. I have a good case. And, as you say, I have a corpse. It becomes my duty to give the courts a man to punish. Latham is good enough. He will keep my record clean."

"And would you jail an innocent man for the sake of your record?"

That was an unnecessary question and Mercado knew it. Gomez was a loyal man—to Gomez. Gomez would jail twenty-seven innocent men to protect his record. At least he had the grace not to deny it. He smiled enigmatically and spread his palms.

"I have spent the day with lawyers," announced Mercado. "I have read old Judge Grannick's will."

"So," said Gomez.

Mercado said: "It seemed his son was cut off because of some criminal record. And his nephew would lose what had been left him if he ever was convicted of a greater crime than the son."

"Common knowledge," said Grannick.

"Moreover," said Mercado, "Ortega, the corpse, was once in jail. And when he died he was broke. Can you put those two facts together, *mi coronel?*"

Gomez wasted no mental effort. He said succinctly: "No."

"Suppose," said Mercado, "that Grannick in his youth served a prison term, unknown to his uncle. Suppose Ortega was in the same prison. Suppose Ortega, knowing the terms of the will, came suddenly upon evil days and needed cash—is it not logical he should try to blackmail Grannick?"

"You have some evidence of this?" said Grannick sharply.

"The evidence of my own intelligence," said Mercado. "According to my researches there was a period of two years in your youth when you were supposed to have run away and shipped out on a freight boat. Those two years coincide with the period that Ortega spent in prison. I do not suppose that you would care to tell me the name of your ship. That would ruin my theory."

There was a long silence. Apparently, Grannick did not care to mention the name of his ship.

"Therefore, I believe," said Mercado, "that you were in the same prison as Ortega and later invented the sea story to prevent your uncle from knowing where you were."

Lamb said, with obvious anxiety: "And you only have the evidence of your own intelligence?"

"Unfortunately," said Mercado. "The records are destroyed. The fingerprints of one Jesus Pinto, which I believe to be an assumed name, are missing. So are most of the other records. His term was served along with Ortega. How much did that cost you, *Señor?*"

Grannick smiled and relief spread itself over the features of Lamb. Gomez voiced their thoughts when he said: "Is that all you have?"

"At the moment," said Mariano Mercado. "Just think it over and you'll see how logical it all is."

Gomez and I thought it over. It may have been logical as hell but the evidence of Mercado's own intelligence wasn't going to work in a courtroom. The more I thought about it the more I was certain Lamb was going to get away with whatever he was doing and I was going to pick oakum or whatever they do to while away the time in a Mexican dungeon.

Gomez took the cigar from his mouth, gave his left mustachio a savage twirl and said: "Let us recapitulate. You are arguing that once, in his youth, Grannick committed a crime. That he kept this fact from his uncle, accounting for his absence by announcing he had been a deckhand.

"In later years, Ortega, who needed cash and served time with Grannick, blackmailed him. Ortega, aware of the terms of the will, insisted Grannick pay him off or he would expose him, thus causing him to lose the fortune."

Mercado nodded. "The will states that if Grannick was ever convicted of a crime greater than that of the deceased's son he shall lose the money; it shall revert to the son's heirs. It's as easy as that."

"Easy?" repeated Gomez dubiously. "I think not, *amigo.* But where does the *señor* Lamb come into this?"

"He is Grannick's heir. The complicated will takes care of every contingency. Lamb's father, an American who is dead, was a friend of old man Grannick's. The will provides that if Alex Grannick here has no issue the money goes to Lamb's issue who is Theodore Lamb over there."

"I still want to know where he comes into it. I believe you charge that Lamb killed Ortega."

Mercado shook his head. I glared at him. I was under the impression that it was the conviction of Lamb which would absolve me. Now Mercado was denying that Lamb had killed Ortega.

"Well, who killed Ortega?" I said.

"Grannick, of course. Then he forced Lamb to try to pin it on someone. Lamb did it willingly enough, knowing he would lose his inheritance if Grannick was sent away for murder. Lamb is no killer. He's a business man. He cheats with his mind, not with a gun."

Grannick cleared his throat from the other end of the room. "It is theory," he said. "Theory pure and simple. You have not made a single statement that would stand up in the most rural court in Mexico."

Lamb nodded in nervous agreement. "Absolutely," he contributed.

I ignored them and watched Gomez. It was his reaction in which I was interested.

Gomez spread two fat palms and shrugged his shoulders. "You've presented a good case," he admitted. "As for me, I'm neutral. I've got to have someone to lock up. All things being equal, I'd prefer Grannick to Latham. Grannick's a Mexican citizen and when we arrest Americans the Embassy always steps in and causes trouble. Now what we need is a confession."

He looked invitingly around the room. He was not at all particular whom he got the confession from. Mercado cleared his throat and said: "You can't get a confession from Latham because he's innocent. You won't get one from Grannick because he's tough."

Both their gazes settled on Lamb who shifted uneasily in his chair.

"A gringo," said Gomez speculatively. *"Gorde cansado."*

"It's worth trying," said Mercado.

Gomez nodded. He crooked a brown finger at Lamb and beckoned. "Come," he said, "we will question you in another room."

LAMB'S FACE was suddenly green. Fury flashed in Grannick's eyes. "You can't do this," he yelled. "It's illegal. Besides Lamb's my guest. I insist—"

"Shut up," said Gomez. He turned to me. "You will remain here and keep an eye on Grannick. Keep him away from telephones. Keep him right in that chair. Come, Señor Lamb."

Señor Lamb, sputtering incoherently, was dragged from his chair into the next room. Mercado followed along after him and Gomez. The door closed behind them, leaving me along with Grannick.

Grannick's eyes were narrowed and his lips set in a thin line. He looked like a professional gambler watching his last grand as the wheel spun. The analogy was not too inaccurate. If Lamb talked he was done. If Lamb held out he retained both freedom and property.

And it was no mere coincidence that I felt exactly the same way. My fate lay with the result of the 'questioning' in the other room no less than did that of Grannick.

Neither of us spoke. The ticking of an ancient grandfather clock was the only sound save that of the storm.

Three quarters of an hour passed by, then the door of the other room opened. Grannick and I glanced up expectantly. Lamb's face was still a dull green. There was a cut over his left eye and a bruise on his cheek. That, I knew, was Gomez' work. But in Lamb's eye there was a glint of triumph.

Mercado appeared with dejection stamped on his brown face. I didn't need to ask any questions. I knew that Theodore Lamb was not as soft as we had thought.

The hall door burst open suddenly and a servant appeared.

"Don Alex," he said to Grannick, "the bridge is down. The storm has carried it away. These *señores* will have to remain here until morning."

Grannick exchanged a glance with Lamb. Lamb nodded almost imperceptibly. Grannick smiled faintly. He said to the *criado:* "Prepare the guest rooms."

The servant left the room. Grannick stood up. "I shall see to the rooms myself," he said. "These servants are not too efficient."

He stalked out, quite assured. Gomez regarded me impersonally. "Well, Latham," he said, "I guess I'll have to take you in again in the morning."

I shot a desperate glance at Mercado. He shook his head sadly. "It is too bad," he said. "We know who committed the crime and why but we cannot prove it. Señor Lamb's cupidity gave him courage. I am now prepared to admit that he has far more courage than I thought only a minute ago."

Lamb said: "Why? What do you mean?"

"You are a brave man," said Mercado, "to sleep in this house tonight."

"Why?"

"Because, though it is true you refused to talk tonight, Grannick has no guarantee that you won't talk tomorrow or the next day or next month. And he is a ruthless man who stops at nothing."

Lamb's face turned slightly green again. "You mean—"

"Only that he may cut your throat while you sleep. Come, Latham, let's find our chamber. I'm sleepy."

I certainly wasn't. However, I went along with him. We met Grannick in the hall and he escorted us into a bedroom that looked like an observatory.

The ceiling was twelve feet high, the walls sixteen feet apart and two huge four poster beds stood in the middle of the room.

Mariano Mercado removed his coat with a preoccupied air. There was an anxious frown on his brow.

I said: "So Lamb didn't crack?"

Mercado shook his head.

"And where does that put me?"

He shrugged. "Not in an enviable position."

"That's just dandy. What do we do now?"

"We'll have another try at Lamb in the morning. In the meantime we'd better pray."

That remark from the lips of such an agnostic as Mariano Mercado caused my heart to sink. If he was relying on Heaven rather than his own wits it didn't seem to me that I had much chance.

I undressed slowly and crawled into bed. Wearing his look of preoccupation and a pair of heliotrope shorts, Mercado did the same.

Long after the light was out I lay on my back staring up at a ceiling I couldn't see. Outside the storm still raged but no more furiously than my own nerves. I heard Mercado snoring gently and it annoyed me unreasonably. The hours marched by on heavy, leaden feet. At last I slept fitfully.

There was a time when I thought I heard stealthy footfalls in the hall. I listened intently but the noise of the wind and rain drowned out all other sound. Then a few moments later I heard the cry.

It was unmistakably a cry from a human throat and it was pregnant with terror. I sprang out of bed reaching for the light switch with one hand and my pants with the other. As I struggled into the latter, I said: "Mercado, didn't you hear—" Then I stopped because his bed was empty.

A MOMENT later I was out in the hall. Gomez, half-dressed, passed me. I followed him to an open door at the end of the passageway. In the room stood Mercado standing over Lamb whose face, this time, was positively verdant.

In the wall over his head was stuck a knife blade with a trembling protruding hilt. In Mercado's hand was the cord of a bathrobe.

"I warned you," said Mercado gravely. "As a matter of fact you owe me your life."

Gomez said: *"Que pasada?"*

"I rather thought Grannick wouldn't take any chances," said Mercado. "I rather thought he might attempt to put Lamb out of the way. So I got out of bed and did sentry go in the dark outside Lamb's door.

"I must have dozed off. When I awakened, Lamb's door was open and a dark figure stood there. I jumped him just as he threw that knife. He squirmed away from me, leaving the cord of his bathrobe in my hand. It's a cinch you'll find there isn't any cord on Grannick's bathrobe right now."

"My Lord," said Lamb and covered his face with his hands. "My Lord, I'll never be safe until he's dead."

"Or in prison," said Mercado. "Why don't you—"

Footfalls sounded in the hall and Grannick's voice cried: "What's the matter? What's going on?"

Lamb seemed to shrink back into the bed. "Keep him away from me," he said. "Don't let him in here. He's a killer. I'll tell you all about him."

Mercado lifted his eyebrows and glanced at Gomez. "You listen to the confession," he said, "I'll keep Grannick away."

He closed the door leaving Lamb and Gomez inside and himself and me in the hallway. Grannick came up to us panting. He was wearing a dressing gown and I observed that he held it together with his hands.

"We will wait in the living room," said Mercado. "Señor Lamb is talking privately to the *coronel*."

"No," shouted Grannick. "You've framed something. I'm going in. I—"

Mercado had a huge revolver in his hand. He thrust its barrel into Grannick's stomach and repeated: "We will wait in the living room."

We marched in there and waited.

Twenty minutes later Gomez appeared with Lamb and three sheets of paper in his hand. He said: "Grannick, as soon as we can cross the stream I'm taking you to jail."

Grannick glared at Lamb and began a string of epithets in two languages. I said: "Mercado, come out to the patio, I want to talk to you a moment."

We stood in the clear dawn on a patio covered with bougainvillea.

"Mercado," I said, "I don't believe Grannick threw that knife. He wouldn't be such a fool. First, suspicion would immediately point to him, second, he wouldn't have hurled it. He would have made sure and stabbed Lamb to death."

"Interesting," murmured Mariano Mercado.

"What I do believe," I went on, "is that you sneaked into Grannick's bedroom, pinched the cord of his robe, went to the kitchen, got a knife and threw it yourself, making sure it hit the wall a foot above Lamb's head. Then you howled and raised the household. When Lamb woke up he helped you howl, only he wasn't kidding."

Mercado regarded me with a faint smile on his lips. "It's an ingenious theory," he said, grinning. "Perhaps it's even true."

Then he suddenly snapped his fingers. "Do you know what I am going to do? Now. *Pronto!*"

I didn't know and I said so.

"Those lovely little *niños* next door. They now inherit the Grannick fortune. I am going over to tell them myself. To tell them what Mariano Mercado has done for them."

He raced out into the dawn. I followed along some twenty feet behind.

In the distance I saw him gain the porch of the cottage. The uniformed guard I had seen the previous evening was still there. As Mercado approached, the guard stretched forth a restraining hand. Mercado, triumphant and excited, thrust it away and crashed through the front door.

The sun had touched the edge of the horizon as I came up to the porch. The guard was exploding Spanish and pointing an indignant finger to an official cardboard poster attached to the side of the house. I read it hastily.

It announced in seventy-two point type that one of the children was afflicted with diphtheria, that the house was under strict quarantine, that no one could leave or enter.

I walked up to the porch and waited. A little later Mercado put a sickly face against the window screen. *"Dios,*

Latham," he said. "The child is ill. The house is quarantined."

I nodded. "The guard tried to tell you that."

"But I?" screamed Mercado. "What will become of me? They won't let me out!"

I grinned. "You stay there until the child is well. There isn't anything to worry about."

"Nothing to worry about!" His voice was a shrill and terrified soprano. "The house is alive with lethal bacteria."

"Don't worry," I said. "I'll go back to town and send out a doctor. He'll give you some shots. I'll get him out right away."

"A doctor!" Mercado's tone was anguished. "Don't waste time sending me a doctor. God knows there is someone I need far more than that. For the love of *Dios,* send me a priest."

THE SHABBY SHROUD

MARIANO MERCADO
FEARLESSLY BRAVED
THE GERM-CLUTTERED
CANTINAS—AND SENT ME
TO THE DUSTY LIBRARY...
TO HUNT A LOVE-STRUCK
MURDERER.

CHAPTER ONE
ANTISEPTIC DICK

MEXICO IS not the ideal country for a guy who makes an occasional valiant effort to stay on the wagon. There are too many *fiestas*. It was four o'clock in the morning and I was no longer quite sure which patron saint I had been so assiduously honoring. Half-a-dozen tourists from Chicago and a handful of us *rentistas* had made the wavering rounds of every *cantina* east of Chapultepec. We were now engaged in officially burying the night with steak and glasses of champagne at *La Cucaracha*.

By now there was an apian buzzing in my head and it seemed that my blood stream contained more alcohol than blood. I swallowed a piece of steak with an effort and looked blinkingly around the room which, oddly enough, was tilted at a thirty degree angle. I was thinking it strange that the glittering bottles did not fall from their seesawing shelves when I suddenly caught sight of Juan Cabajal in the midst of a merry group at the bar.

I recalled dimly that I had seen Cabajal at least twice before that evening. Now, to see Juan Cabajal in three different bars in the course of one night was not at all unusual. The remarkable aspect was that on each occasion he had appeared to be paying for the drinks. At the moment he was jabbering rapid Spanish and gesticulating wildly with both hands, in one of which he held a bottle

"If anyone comes near—I'll
cut this man's throat."

of expensive champagne, in the other a fist full of hundred
peso notes.

Juan Cabajal was a flashily dressed youth, something
under thirty years of age, with a furtive manner and a face
the color of muddy coffee. His complexion, however, was
by no means as dark as his reputation.

Cabajal was a grade-A murmurer and a first-class hand kisser of my unescorted countrywomen. For him there was money in it. But not enough to warrant his flashing a fat bankroll and buying drinks for the competition in his own racket.

As I pondered this with alcoholic gravity, Cabajal caught my eye. *"Ai!"* he cried. "The *señor* Latham. You must have a drink."

He snatched a glass from the bar and weaved toward me, still clutching the champagne bottle. I eyed him owlishly and said, "Have you inherited a Taxco silver mine?"

"No," he said excitedly. "Something better. A Gringo. A luscious blonde Gringo. We are to elope at any minute. I have a pair of tickets in my pocket."

"Oh," I said, "so you're getting married and you've bought tickets for the honeymoon?"

He looked at me as if I had accused him of knocking his mother's teeth in. "I marry no gringo," he said indignantly. "And *she* bought the tickets."

"Oh," I said again. "You've got a real sucker this time. A recent arrival?"

"She's been here for three or four months. We shall travel for a year or so at her expense. Then I shall return. Without her."

"But with her money?"

He didn't get a chance to answer that. His companions at the bar had become thirsty again, and there was no point in buying their own drinks while Cabajal still held a handful of hundred peso notes. They took him bodily away from me.

I looked over at the bar. It was now tilted at an angle of forty-five degrees. I figured I'd better get to bed before it turned completely over.

IT WAS three o'clock in the afternoon when I awoke. My thirst was the most prodigious thing this side of the Sahara and a diabolical drum was pounding just behind my throbbing temples.

I got out of bed warily, drank a quart of orange juice and a pint of coffee and proceeded to dress. I had a little trouble shaving and fastening the buttons on my shirt. However, by the time I stepped into the street I was sure I felt infinitely better than any of the visiting firemen from Chicago.

I hailed a cab and headed for Mariano Mercado's.

I entered his austere and sanitary apartment which made the average hospital ward resemble a germ trap. The chairs in the living room were of enameled metal. The windows were devoid of curtains and there was not a cushion in sight. The floor was uncarpeted and highly polished.

Mercado sat behind a thoroughly disinfected desk whose top supported a square sheet of virginal blotting paper and a phalanx of bottles. Ten minutes after science discovered a medicine, a sample of it was on Mercado's desk. Drug stores and chemical companies loved him. Indiscriminately he bought everything from snake oil to the latest variation of penicillin.

I greeted him, said, "You should have come along with us last night. It was quite an evening."

He looked at me with a touch of fear in his brown, liquid eyes. "I intended to. But I coughed. At six minutes past seven I coughed. Naturally, I had to look after myself."

He glanced at his watch, snatched up an atomizer and squirted green liquid into his throat. I sighed. If Mariano Mercado had coughed at six minutes past seven last night I was going to have a trying day. For a cough to Mercado was what galloping consumption was to anyone else.

He was a little brown man with a shrewd mind, a great deal of physical courage where bacteria was not concerned; a taste for clothing loud as a thunderbolt, and a fearful hypochondria. He had devoted the thirty-odd years of his life conducting a defensive warfare against germs.

"Latham," he said, leaning over the desk, "have you any idea how many germs lurk in a human thorax during the incubation period of a common cold?"

"Millions," I said hastily. "Have we anything on for today in the matter of private detecting? If not, I—"

"Millions!" he snorted. "Millions, indeed. Latham, do you know what a googol is?"

I didn't know what a googol was but I was very much afraid I was going to find out in several thousand portentous words. The bell saved me.

It rang sharply in the outer wall. Gratefully, I got out of my uncomfortable chair and went down the well scrubbed passageway to meet whatever diversion offered. On the threshold I found the squat, swarthy figure of *El coronel* Gomez of the local *policia*. For once in my life I was glad to see him. Anything was preferable to hearing the thousandth version of Mariano Mercado's alarmed views on bacteria.

I led Gomez along the hall to the living room and waved him to a chair.

Now the affection which existed between Mariano Mercado, *detectivo particular,* and *Coronel* Gomez of the Federal District Police was by no means the affection of Romeo and Juliet. Gomez was principally interested in the financial fortunes of Gomez. Mercado was a rigidly honest man.

Gomez possessed a politician's instinct for nosing out the location of a buck. To him a peso was a peso whether its background was extra-legal or not. He was fat, oily, slow witted and heavy handed. Mercado was none of these things and Gomez resented it. He resented even more the fact that on more than one occasion Mercado had arrested a killer and collected his fee before Gomez had even been apprised of the murder.

Therefore, it rather surprised me when in response to Mercado's cool, "Good day," Gomez beamed, tugged at his moustachios and said with the utmost cordiality, "And how is my *amigo*, today? In the best of health, I presume.

Ah, if you were ill or incapacitated, the law enforcement agencies of the city would suffer a dolorous blow."

Gomez shook his head and sighed mournfully as if the very thought of Mercado's non-existent illness was something too painful to be borne. Mercado blinked suspiciously and lighted a mentholated cigarette.

"I am nothing if not frank," said Gomez, which was as large a lie as I had heard since the demise of Herr Doktor Goebbels. "Therefore, I shall say that I need your help. The city needs your help. The nation needs it. *Two* nations need it."

He stopped short of the universe, took an ebony cigar from his pocket and chewed it thoughtfully.

"Naturally," he went on, "I would not ask a man of your talents to aid me for nothing. I offer you five hundred pesos for the use of your brain."

I was all ears. If Gomez's cordiality surprised me, his willingness to part with money—especially five hundred pesos—was a bolt from the blue.

Mercado blinked and said, "You fascinate me. What has happened?"

"A girl is missing," said Gomez. "I will pay five hundred pesos for your help. However, for the sake of the morale of the police department, I must have your word that I will get all the credit if you find her."

That made it clearer. I guessed there were glory and kudoes, perhaps even promotion, if Gomez found the missing girl. Doubtless, he had decided that whatever he got out of it was worth much more than five hundred pesos. However we still could use five hundred pesos.

"It sounds like a reasonable offer," said Mercado. "Tell me what you know about this girl."

"A gringo," said Gomez. "A blonde gringo. Her family has money. She has been working in the city as the secretary to an American writer, one Professor Workin. Last night she disappeared, leaving a note behind her. Here is the note."

He withdrew a vast leather wallet from his tunic, extracted a piece of paper and handed it to Mercado. I got up and read it over his shoulder.

> I know that you and others who love me will be shocked at what I am about to do. However, in certain matters one must use one's own judgement. Romantic love is a greater force than all other kinds. So I am going away with my knight. Don't worry and forgive me.

It was written on a small, uneven piece of paper which apparently had been torn from a larger sheet. It was in sprawling feminine handwriting and it was unsigned.

"Her name," said Gomez, "is Isabel Scott. She has probably fallen in love with some *valiente* who has run off with her because of her money."

THE WORD *valiente* in Spanish may mean exactly what it sounds like or it can be spoken ironically to indicate a two-bit braggart along the lines of Juan Cabajal. Cabajal, with a handful of dough, boasting of the gringo blonde he was about to run away with and Gomez with a police report of a missing girl fitted together much too well to be purely coincidental. However, I had no intention of opening my mouth until Gomez had laid his five hundred pesos on the sanitary desk.

Mercado handed Gomez back the note and said, "Have you checked the handwriting?"

Gomez nodded. "It is undoubtedly the handwriting of Isabel Scott. Now, will you help me?"

Mercado nodded slowly. "For five hundred pesos, I shall help you. But first I want to know why should you pay cash from your own pocket to solve a routine police case?"

Gomez adopted an expression of smug righteousness. "Patriotism," he said. "To aid the good-neighbor policy. The American Embassy is worried. To find this girl will cement relations between our country and the United States. In this world of chaos, it is a beneficial thing if two countries can—"

For the second time that morning the doorbell rang, thus saving me from listening to a dull and obviously phony speech. I clattered along the antiseptic floor to the front door, still wondering why Gomez was handing out five hundred pesos.

On the other side of the door stood a blond lad of about twenty-four. He wore no hat and his hair was awry. His face was flushed and he spoke with an excited Indiana accent.

"I want to see Mercado," he said. "They tell me he's the smartest detective in Mexico. He's *got* to do something."

I led him into the living room, asked him his name and indicated Mercado. He ignored Gomez, faced the bottle-decorated desk, and speech bubbled from his lips.

"My name's Rolland. Roger Rolland. Student at the University of Mexico. My fiancée is missing. You've got to find her. I've no faith in these coppers, even if her family is offering five thousand bucks to the policeman who finds her. I want an independent investigation. I'll offer you—"

Mercado held up a slim, scrubbed hand. "Is the name of your fiancée Isabel Scott?"

"Yes. And I—"

Mercado silenced him again. He shifted his gaze to Gomez. Gomez found something of intense interest in his manicure. He studied the nails of his left hand with admirable concentration.

"Patriotism," murmured Mercado. "Good-neighbor policy. In this world of chaos no price, not even five hundred pesos, is too much to pay for happy international relations."

Gomez looked up. He had the grace to blush. He said, "I assure you—"

"I assure *you*," said Mercado, "that I will solve this case not because of amicable international relations, not because of my sense of justice, but only to see that you do not collect that five thousand dollars."

Gomez picked his bulk out of the chair and waddled sheepishly down the hall like a little boy caught red handed in the jam pot.

"Now," said Mercado to Rolland, "sit down, calm yourself, and state your case."

Rolland sat down, talked, but failed signally to calm himself.

"Workin, the guy she works for, saw her yesterday. She's helping him compile an anthology of short stories. She didn't show up this morning and he found this note from her. He notified the coppers. I think these coppers are dopes. I want you to look into it. Here, I stopped at the bank and brought a retainer. Here's a few thousand pesos."

He handed a wad of blue bank notes to Mercado who shuddered. The number of germs which took up residence on old bills was legion. Mercado would have touched a leper as quickly as he would handle a bank note. I had no such scruples. I took the cash and counted it. It was the equivalent of one thousand American dollars.

"This will do nicely," I said. "Go on."

He shrugged. "I didn't know she was missing until a little while ago. I never wanted her to come here anyway, but she was crazy to travel. Her family let her go as long as she was working for the professor. They thought he'd keep an eye on her. Just to be near her I transferred from my college in the States to the University of Mexico."

Mercado looked at him shrewdly. "Did her family know that you were engaged?"

Rolland shook his head. "No one knew but us. Her family is quite wealthy. They don't think I have enough money to marry her. For heaven's sake will you do something? Lord knows what's happened to her by now."

"Very well," said Mercado, "I shall make an investigation. I shall see the professor and find out everything I can. Leave me your address and I'll call you if I discover anything."

I drew a deep breath. For years Mercado had been the mastermind and I the stooge. Invariably he held back information on me. But this time I had something. I had Cabajal.

"Rolland," I said, "pull yourself together. I guarantee that we'll have some information for you by tomorrow morning. As a matter of fact I almost have this thing figured right now. I just want to check before I make a definite statement."

Rolland looked at me gratefully. Mercado stared in utter amazement. His opinion of my deductive abilities was not precisely as high as the Empire State Building.

I said, "Rolland, you're sure she loved you? Sure she wouldn't have gone off with another man?"

"Of course, she loved me. Oh, I know what you're talking about. The cops hold that theory. They told me she said as much in the note she left. But it's a lie. That note's a phony."

I waved him toward the door. "Very well. We will give you some information in the morning."

He nodded and left.

CHAPTER TWO
THE INFERNAL
TRIANGLE

MERCADO GAVE me a dirty look. "Well," he said stiffly, "when you go downtown tomorrow to find that girl you can bank that money at the same time."

I grinned at him. He was nettled, believing I'd figured something out before he had. "Don't you want to hear my theory?"

"What is it?"

"That dame has run away with Juan Cabajal. They left town sometime between four this morning and whenever that note was found. She wasn't as nuts about Rolland as he thought."

"Are you playing thousand-to-one shots or do you know something?"

"I know something." I told him of meeting Cabajal at La Cucaracha the night before. He became more amiable as he realized I'd been merely lucky, not brilliant.

"Well," he said when I'd finished, "it's simple enough, then. We'll check the place where Cabajal lived. Maybe we can pick up the trail there. If not, we can check around the steamship companies, the railroads and the buses. Since he said he had the tickets we can't very well miss. Wait until I change my clothes."

He went into the bedroom, emerging some twenty minutes later clad like a more daring type of rainbow. His suit was a bright, jealous green and it had been cut by a scissors which flouted tradition. The jacket had a single button in the front and an even dozen on each sleeve. His shoes were yellow as the proverbial dog and his shirt pink as an embarrassed salmon's underbelly. His tie was utterly beyond my vocabulary to describe.

He used his atomizer once more before venturing into the warm air of the city, wrapped his scrawny neck carefully in a woolen muffler and donned a chocolate brown topcoat.

As we went downstairs, he said, "Do you know where Cabajal lives?"

"We can find out in half the saloons and all the dance halls. We'll try La Paloma first."

Since *hombres* like Cabajal have percentage deals with half the bartenders in town to telephone them whenever a group of feminine tourists who looked like good business come into the cantina, I was by no means surprised when I obtained the address on my first try.

We then drove a couple of miles toward Xochomilco and the cab pulled up at a battered stone house.

A sullen fat man at the desk said he didn't know whether or not the *señor* Cabajal was in. He indicated that he didn't care either. However, he gave us the room number and we mounted a dark staircase which was indubitably alive with bacteria. Mercado buried his brown nose in his muffler.

I knocked on a door whose paint was flaking. Save for the echo of my own knuckles down the dark corridor there was no answer. As I knocked a second time Mercado took his nose out of his muffler long enough to say, "Maybe the door's open. If you're right, he's far away by now, but I'd like to look over the room."

The knob turned. I went into the shabby room with Mercado behind me. Mercado looked across the room at the sagging bed and said, "He *is* in. He's asleep."

I got to the bed first. I took one look. Cabajal was in, all right. At least his body was.

I flung back the dirty comforter which covered him. Behind me Mercado grunted and said, "It's not pretty."

It wasn't. Cabajal was stripped to the waist, still wearing his shoes and trousers. He lay flat on his back staring at the cracked ceiling. His skull had been smashed to pulp.

There was no mystery about the weapon. It was a thick, green-glass tequila bottle lying on the floor by the head of the bed. The paper of its label was as bloody as was Cabajal's head. On the scuffed carpet near it were half-a-dozen hundred peso notes.

Mercado came closer and peered at the body, being most careful to permit nothing in the room to touch his own scoured person.

He said, "He's been dead for some time. I'd guess twelve hours. We must examine everything in the room. But carefully. We don't want any possible fingerprints smudged."

I said, "We?" with ironic intonation. I was quite aware that this was a solo job. Mariano Mercado would rather have faced all the atomic bombs in the stock pile than touch a single object in this filthy room. I sighed, took a handkerchief from my pocket and embarked upon a comprehensive frisk.

The room yielded nothing illuminating. In the pocket of the dead man's coat which hung behind the door, I found a wallet. It contained some money, a few scented visiting cards and a steamship ticket to Patagonia in an envelope.

I said, "He was supposed to sail today. At dawn. Obviously he didn't. However, there's only one ticket here. If he intended taking the girl there should be two."

Mercado's eyes were black and thoughtful above the edge of his muffler. He said, "Be careful of that ticket. I want Gomez to look it over for fingerprints."

I nodded and put the ticket back in the envelope. I said, "You think the girl sailed alone?"

Mercado shook his head dreamily.

"Then after she discovered that Cabajal didn't turn up, why didn't she go back home?"

"A fair question," said Mercado, "which I can't answer. Go tell Gomez Cabajal is dead. Ask him to look the ticket and its envelope over for fingerprints."

"Whose do you think he'll find other than Cabajal's?"

Mercado shook his head again. "I don't even think he'll find Cabajal's. Meet me at the office as soon as you can and we'll call on this man, Workin. I have to have a bath immediately."

A well fed cockroach waddled across the frayed carpet and began a slow ascent of Mercado's polished shoe. He regarded it with horror. He kicked out frantically, dislodging the insect, then turned and fled down the stairs as if a platoon of the more vicious Furies were chasing after him.

I descended with more decorum and took a taxi over to Police Headquarters.

IT WAS dusk when we arrived at the place where Workin lived. It was a few miles beyond the city limits on the Cuernavaca road. The house was a two-story stone job with a rock fence in front of it. In its day it had evidently been quite a *casa grande*. But now it was in a state of weary dilapidation. At the rear, the stone fence sank exhaustedly to the ground and the back yard, which must have been all of five acres, was unprotected save at its very end where a wide stream ran parallel with the road.

Mercado told the taxi to wait, as we mounted a ramshackle porch and tugged at an old-fashioned bell.

The *criada* who opened the door was a fat woman of full Indian blood. She seemed relieved to see us. When we asked for Workin she shook her head and said, *"El señor esta borracho, muy borracho."*

I stepped across the threshold and the servant's information that Workin was drunk was corroborated forthwith. The hall stank of rum. It was as if we stood in a great wind which was rolling off a rum plant.

The woman threw open a door at the end of the corridor, gestured us through and retreated hastily.

The room we entered was used as an office. Two desks were against the wall, one of them holding a typewriter. A long table in the center of the chamber was covered with scattered manuscripts. On one of the desks were three full bottles of rum and half a dozen empties. At its side was a worn swivel chair and sagging in it was William Workin.

He was a thin man with a corvine nose, white hair and sunken cheeks. His brown eyes were bloodshot. He held a glass in his hand and as I drew nearer I discovered that his breath was such to make Bacchus avert his head.

Mercado said, "Good evening," in his perfect, unaccented English and stated the purpose of our visit. At the mention of Isabel Scott's name, Workin grabbed the edge of the desk and pulled the swivel chair upright.

"A tragedy," he said, drunkenly dramatic. "That innocent young girl eloping with some scum of the town. I dare not face her family. It's a frightful thing. I can not stand it."

He uttered a weird howling sound, let go of the desk, and the back of the chair dropped toward the floor. Workin went back with it. He lifted his glass, slopped rum over his shirt as he drank it.

Mercado looked at him long and hard. Then his sharp gaze moved about the room. It riveted at last upon the typewriter. He went over to it and touched the space bar with his gloved finger.

There was no answering click and the carriage failed to move.

"Ah," said Mercado, "the typewriter is broken?"

Workin pulled himself upright again. "Yeah," he said. "Busted spring or something, Gotta get it fixed." He uncorked a live bottle with his teeth and poured himself a handsome slug.

Mercado said, "When did it happen?"

Workin looked up, blinked and said, "Huh? Oh, the typewriter? Yesterday morning I think. Gotta get it fixed. You guys want a drink?"

Mercado didn't answer him. His little eyes darted about the room. I, no gifthorse examiner, helped myself to a moderate portion.

Mercado said, "You're compiling some sort of anthology, aren't you?"

Workin nodded without looking up from his glass.

"I don't see any books around here," said Mercado. "Save for that dictionary there and the Thesaurus."

"Just took a batch back to the library," said Workin. "I get what I want from the American library over there on the *Reforma*." He paused for a moment, then said brokenly, "When I think of that poor kid—hell, I don't dare get sober again." He drained his glass, replaced it on the desk and reached for the bottle again.

Mercado stared at the glass which was none too clean. "Drink from the bottle," he said.

Workin gaped at him and said, "Huh?"

"Drink from the bottle," said Mercado. "These servants never sterilize glasses properly. You run less risk if you drink from the bottle."

Workin was still bewildered. "Less risk of what?" he asked wonderingly.

"Germs," said Mercado impatiently. "Disease. Have you the faintest conception of how many germs can exist on the edge of a dirty glass? May I tell you—"

Workin, I was sure, still didn't understand. But he saw it was one hell of a good idea without listening to the reasons.

"Damn good thought," he said. "Drink from the bottle. Save time." He snatched up the rum and tilted it to his lips. His grip on the desk slipped again and the back of the chair plunged down. Workin didn't miss a swallow.

Mariano Mercado strode toward the door without bothering to bid our host good night. The *criada* was in the hall. He gave her a five-peso note and asked, "The *señor* drinks a lot, eh?"

She shook her head. "Not at all until now. Occasionally, he would drink some beer. But ever since the secretary has run away he has done nothing but drink rum."

We went back to our waiting taxi and headed toward Mexico City.

"Well," I said, "where are we now? Do we know anything?"

"Not much. There is a lot of routine checking to do."

"When do we do it?"

"We don't. Let Gomez do it. It's his job. We can find out what we need to know from *la policia*."

"If there's no work to do," I said, "let's spend some of that fee Rolland gave us looking over the better bars."

Mercado shook his head. "No. You have work early in the morning. You are to go to the American library, get a list of every book Workin has withdrawn, and read them."

I am not a man who enjoys wallowing in work. I stared at him unhappily. "He may have taken out dozens of books. You mean I have to read them all?"

"Not all. Only those either written by an Englishman or published in England."

"And what am I looking for?"

"You will know that immediately when you find it. I should like to get done by tomorrow afternoon. You had better go home to bed."

"All right," I said without enthusiasm. "And what about you?"

He smiled at me. "I? I shall spend some of Rolland's fee investigating those better bars you spoke of."

"All right," I said. "But I hope they serve your drink in an unwashed glass that a typhus case has just finished with."

He was still staring at me in outraged horror when I got out of the cab and climbed the steps to my apartment.

ALL THE following morning I spent immersed in some rather dull books. I ate a light lunch and resumed my task. I ceased at precisely twelve minutes past three, at which time I jammed on my hat, thrust a copy of *The Purple Lady,* published by R.A. Rogers of London in 1916, under my arm, and dashed off in a state of febrile excitement to Mercado's apartment.

As I entered he was waving at a most intelligent fly with a flit gun. I speak of the fly's mentality because only a most elite fly could ever have figured out how to break through the fine wire defences that screened Mercado's windows.

At last he brought it down in a gray cloud of spray, stamped on it heavily, swept it into a dust pan and interred it in the garbage pail.

I threw the book on the desk and said with grudging admiration, "It's on page 135. How on earth did you know?"

He said, "I'll tell you something else," ignoring the fact that he'd told me nothing at all yet. "I've spoken to Gomez on the telephone. There were no fingerprints at all on Cabajal's ticket nor the envelope where you found them."

I wrinkled my brow. "There must be some fingerprints, even if they're undecipherable, on anything—unless someone wipes them off."

"Precisely," said Mercado. "Moreover, Gomez checked at Cabajal's hotel. He's holding that fat clerk as a material witness. I don't think it'll do him much good. The man says he's away from the desk a lot and all kinds of people are going in and out. He swears he saw no one suspicious go up to Cabajal's room." His manner was smug. It was obvious he knew more than Gomez or I did.

I said, "Well, what do we do now?"

"You go down to the University and bring back Rolland. I think we'll need him. In the meantime I will call my archeologist friend, Professor Palacios." I wrinkled my brow at that. Palacios was an archeologist of reputation. He held a Government job in charge of all digging in the Federal District. Archeology in Mexico is big time stuff. Someone is always finding priceless pieces of stone left by the Aztecs.

"What on earth has Palacios to do with this?"

"I'm going to ask him to do us a favor," said Mercado. "It may save a lot of time."

I inferred from all this that he was in his non-talking mood, which in turn meant that he was just about ready to come up with a solution to the mystery. I shrugged my shoulders and went out of the house as he picked up the phone and asked for the Government Department of Archeology.

I returned about an hour later with an excited Rolland who plied me with questions during the trip. Unfortunately, I couldn't answer them.

Upon our arrival Mercado had divested himself of the royal purple bathrobe he had been wearing and caparisoned his little body in an elegant suit fashioned of brown-and-yellow checks, a shirt of a torchy blue and a natty pair of two-color shoes.

Despite his eager desire for information Rolland took a moment out to blink. After his recovery, he said, "Mr. Mercado, have you any news for me? Do you know where Isabel is?"

"Not exactly," said Mercado. "But I hope to know tonight."

"Good. But you must let me give you more money. The thousand was only a retainer. For a complete job you're entitled to more."

Mercado eyed him oddly and shook his head. "No," he said in a strained voice, "you've already paid me enough."

That struck me as rather odd. Mercado was not a slow man with a buck. He wasn't frugal. But on the other hand it was unlike him to turn down a fee honestly earned and voluntarily offered.

"I have some money," said Rolland. "I can afford it."

This time Mercado didn't answer him at all. Instead he picked up the book I had brought. He handed it to Rolland and said, "Turn to page 135. Paragraph three."

Rolland did as he was told. Mercado said, "Read it. Read it aloud."

"I know that you and others who love me will be shocked at what I am about to do. However, in certain matters one must use one's own judgement. Romantic love is a—" Rolland broke off suddenly. His face was pale and there was utter astonishment in his eyes. "My Lord! That's what Isabel wrote in that note before she disappeared. I saw it printed in *Universal.*"

"Right," said Mercado, "and Workin's typewriter was broken that morning."

Rolland dropped the book from limp fingers. I thought for a moment that his eyes would bulge from his head. His face was cold and lethal and murder was written indelibly upon it. He said frozenly, "What do you mean?"

MERCADO SAID quietly, "As I see it, you were not the only man who loved Isabel Scott."

"You mean that scum, Cabajal?"

Mercado shook his head. "Cabajal never even met her. I mean Workin."

"Workin? That old fool? She could never have loved him."

"More's the pity," murmured Mercado.

"That's why he killed her."

"Killed her?" gasped Rolland. "You mean she's dead?"

In a way Mercado's statement made some sense to me; in another it did not. "If he loved her, why should he kill her?" I asked.

"Why not?" said Mercado. "You have the superficial romantic viewpoint of your countrymen. If he loved her he had all the reason in the world for killing her as long as she did not love him. Half the killings in Mexico are committed for that very reason. The fact that he embarked on that sudden drunken orgy gave me the idea."

Rolland seemed stunned. He muttered rather irrelevantly, "I thought that Workin didn't drink."

"He didn't," said Mercado. "Then he suddenly goes on a terrific bender. As a friend of the girl, of her family, it is reasonable that he would be upset. But upset to the point of drinking up all the rum in the world? No. Only a lover would feel that way."

"Or a murderer," I said.

"Especially a combination of both," said Mercado.

Rolland spoke as if with a tremendous effort. "What's all this business about that disappearance note? And why are the same words in that book?"

"Because," said Mercado, "Isabel copied them from the book which Workin happened to have in the house at the time. He told her that he loved her. She apparently turned him down. She also told him she was going to marry another man. Workin resolved no one should have her if he couldn't. He plotted to kill her."

I asked, "How did he get her to write that note?"

"It was simple. He deliberately broke the typewriter. He told her he wanted something copied at once. With the typewriter out of order, Isabel naturally copied it in longhand. Workin tore the words he didn't need off the page and kept the part about the elopement."

"Yes," I said, "but what of Cabajal?"

"That was part of the plan. Before he killed her, Workin got in touch with Cabajal. If he knew Cabajal at all, he knew he could be bought. Cabajal was presented with a sum of money and a ticket on condition he boast around town that he was eloping with Isabel and that he use the ticket the next day and keep out of the way until the whole affair had been forgotten."

It made sense now. "And in that way," I said, "no one would ever accuse Workin of murder."

"No one would ever suspect murder had been done."

"How did you ever figure this out? Especially the part about the book?"

Mercado shrugged with false modesty. "The spelling. Now, Isabel Scott was an educated American girl. Yet she spelled judgement with an *e*. That is an English spelling, not an American one. That argued she had been copying from something. The fact of the broken typewriter clinched it."

"Wait a minute," said Rolland and his voice was cracked ice. "It's a nice theory. It's an ingenious theory. And I completely believe it. But can you prove it? Can you even prove there has been a murder? Can you find the body?"

"I hope," said Mercado, "that Workin will find it for us."

"When?" said Rolland. "How long will we have to wait?"

Mercado glanced at the watch on his slim wrist. "A few hours, if I've guessed right. When it gets dark we're going out to his house. Unless he has disposed of the body in some other manner than the one I've figured, we should be able to prove our case tonight."

I was becoming rather bewildered again. "How do you figure he has disposed of the body?"

"I believe he has buried it on his property," said Mercado. "Perhaps he removed it. If so, it'll take us longer to track it down. But the obvious thing would be to bury it on that acreage behind his house."

"Heavens," I said. "You mean we've got to dig up five acres tonight?"

Mercado smiled and shook his head. "No. I'm banking on Workin digging the body up for us."

"But why?" asked Rolland. "Why should that rat—?"

At this point Mercado coughed. It was not a racking cough. It was not a harsh, vibrant cough. It was a slight, discreet irritation of the throat. Its effect, however, was electric.

Mercado's face paled to the color of coffee grounds which have been used four times. He blinked hastily and muttered a Spanish oath. His tan and trembling hand stretched forth and grabbed a bottle of pills. He spilled three of these into his palm and swallowed them like a camel drinking water after ten arid days.

He grabbed one of the atomizers, opened his mouth and pumped as if he were putting out a fire. Then he leaned back in his chair with an expression which would have brought a tear of pity to the eye of a bronze statue.

"Duty," he said with calm resignation, "it will kill me."

Rolland, who knew nothing of his hypochondriacal trend, looked at him in amazement and said, "What are you talking about?"

"I should never go out in the night air," said Mercado. "It will doubtless mean my death. But duty demands it. There is a killer to be trapped."

"It was only a little cough," I said.

Mercado laughed bravely. "A little cough," he repeated. "Just a little cough. Do either of you gentlemen possess any tubercular statistics? I can tell you some awful things."

He took a deep breath and began to talk. They were awful things, indeed.

CHAPTER THREE
BURY THE DEAD

IT WAS ten o'clock last night when we left Mercado's apartment in a borrowed car. The moon had not yet risen and the stars were obscured by clouds.

Mercado, who was driving, halted the car at the side of the road a good kilometer from Workin's house. He handed Rolland and myself flashlights and said, "Follow me and be careful. We may have to wait some time. Don't turn on those lights until I tell you to."

We moved cautiously through the darkness. The air was warm and the grass springy underfoot. As far as I could figure it out we were making a sort of flanking movement on Workin's place, a maneuver which would bring us out at the rear of the house.

At last Mercado came to an abrupt halt. From somewhere nearby odd noises came to my ear. There was an occasional clinking sound followed by a soft and somehow familiar drumming. I heard Mercado inhale sibilantly.

"Ready with the lights?" he whispered. *"Bueno!"* Turn them on."

Our thumbs flicked against the metal buttons. Three yellow beams thrust themselves through the darkness and converged in a single golden halo some thirty yards distant.

I blinked at the eerie sight etched brilliantly against my eyes.

Standing blinded, as if looking directly at the sun, was William Workin. He stood over an oblong pit in the earth and he leaned on a long-handled shovel. He was coatless and he wore no hat. His gray hair was awry and his drunken, bloodshot eyes held terror and apprehension in their depths. Sweat ran down his face and as we advanced I could hear his heavy breathing.

I moved closer until I was at the edge of the excavation. It was about four feet deep and at its bottom there protruded from the earth one end of a burlap bag. There was something lumpy inside.

I shuddered. This time I was in no need of any explanation from Mariano Mercado. I knew that the pit where I stood was a grave, the burlap bag a shabby shroud.

Workin, who had been glaring at us defiantly, suddenly bent his head. Choking sobs issued from his throat.

"I loved her," he said brokenly. "I was mad. I couldn't bear the thought of anyone else marrying her."

I felt Rolland tense at my side. I heard him utter an obscene word. I grabbed his shoulder as he moved toward Workin. Mercado looked at him oddly.

He said, "The law will deal with Workin. Not you."

Rolland said harshly, "The law! You haven't even got capital punishment in Mexico."

"Ah," said Mercado, "do you believe that murderers should die?"

Rolland hesitated for a long moment. He said at last, "I believe he should die."

"Then you condemn yourself to death," said Mercado.

There was a long, strange pause. The moon climbed up in the sky and cast an argent light over the lovely Mexican plateau. Rearing darkly against the sky, the Sleeping Woman stood massively to the south. Workin stopped weeping abruptly.

Rolland said, "I condemn myself to death?" biting off each word viciously.

"Porque no?" said Mercado. "For you, too, are a murderer."

Rolland drew a deep breath. His hand hovered very close to his hip pocket and I stiffened. However, he made no overt move. Mercado flicked off his flash. He looked a bright-eyed gnome in the moonlight. When he spoke it sounded more like a soliloquy than if he was directly addressing us.

"Many men might have killed Juan Cabajal," he said. "The sort of people he knew might kill him for a hundred peso note or less. Yet whoever killed him did not take the hundred peso notes which were there for the taking.

"Many of those who might have murdered Cabajal would have gone through his wallet. The bolder ones would have taken that steamship ticket and tried to get a refund for it. The more timid would destroy it. Neither of them would carefully wipe off the fingerprints and return it to the wallet."

Rolland rasped, "You fool, what are you trying to say?"

"THAT YOU heard, or at least heard about, Cabajal's boasting that he was eloping with your girl. That you found out where he lived, went there and quarrelled with him. You killed him. Then you found he had but one steamship ticket. That struck you as odd. But you reasoned perhaps he had already given Isabel her ticket, so you waited, waited for her to keep her tryst for the elopement. She never came."

Had I not been so engrossed in Mercado's narrative, I would, perhaps, have paid more attention to the hopeful gleam in Workin's eye, to the grim intensity of Roger Rolland.

"No," said Mercado, "she never came. So Rolland left the corpse of the man he had killed and looked for her. He found she was missing, that she had left a note which bore out the story that she was to ran away with Cabajal. Rolland was baffled. So baffled that he drew five thousand pesos from the bank and engaged a *detectivo particular* to find Isabel Scott."

He stopped for a moment, took a step toward the grave and gestured gracefully, "There she is!"

"You were lucky," said Rolland, and from his tone I knew his throat was dry with fear. "You were lucky with Workin. You only had an unprovable theory until you happened to find him digging up the body tonight."

"Lucky?" said Mercado, a note of amusement in his voice. "Workin, will you tell us why you have engaged in this macabre nocturnal task?"

"I had to," said Workin hoarsely. "The Department of Archeology phoned me today. They told me they were going to start digging on this property tomorrow. They believe there's some old Aztec stuff here. I knew if they found the body I'd be suspected. I wanted to get it out of the way before morning."

"That was my friend," said Mercado to Rolland. "The *señor* Palacios of the Archeological Department. I asked him to call, to tell this lie for me."

"All right," said Rolland in a flat voice, "so you weren't lucky. You can prove a murder on Workin. You can't prove one on me."

Mercado shrugged. "I can not. I am a man of honor. But the *coronel* Gomez will prove it all right."

"How can he?"

"When I tell him my theory he will believe it. For a handful of pesos and a few blows his material witness will swear he saw you enter the hotel. Gomez may get other witnesses by the same methods if he needs them."

Mercado sighed sadly as if he were pained beyond all endurance at the extra-legal methods of the *coronel* Gomez. And it was then that Workin sprang.

He seized Mercado with his left hand and whipped a knife from his pocket with his right. It was a long knife with a rusted blade and a jagged edge. I was about to move in on him when a bloodcurdling shriek left Mercado's lips.

For a moment I thought Workin had slashed his throat. Save in the matter of bacteria Mercado possessed as much physical courage as any man I know. But now as Workin held the knife two inches from his throat, Mercado's head was drawn back. There was panic and ineffable dread in his eyes. His face was no longer brown. Horror had rendered it a dirty gray.

"If anyone comes near—" yelled Workin—"I shall cut this man's throat."

I moved toward them. Mercado said in a cracked and high-pitched voice, "For heaven's sake keep away, Latham. Find out what he wants and give it to him."

I stood frozen with indecision. Rolland said, "I'm not going to stand by and see that killer get away with murdering Isabel no matter if he does nick Mercado."

Mercado uttered a despairing groan.

Workin lifted his voice hysterically, "Rolland, you fool, this is your chance as well as mine. You killed Cabajal. You'll rot in a Mexican jail along with me. Join forces with me now. Let's escape. Let's get over the Honduras border. You can settle your differences with me later."

The moon was now high in the sky. Its bland silver light cast itself about the crazy scene. Mercado looking like a ghost, staring with horror at the knife blade; Workin standing over him like some mad priest above a sacrificial altar; Rolland, a thoughtful frown on his young face, slowly reaching in his hip pocket.

"Workin," he said, "it's a working alliance until we hit the border. Then heaven help you."

"What'll we do with the two of them?" said Workin.

"Tie 'em up. Here a knife's no good. I've got a gun. You go to the house and get some rope, a clothes line, something."

HE TOOK an automatic from his pocket, pushed Workin aside, took up a position a few feet to Mercado's side and covered us both with his gun.

As Workin thrust his knife back into his pocket I saw the grayness fade from Mercado's face and the color flood back into it. He squared his thin shoulders.

"Hurry up, Workin, get some rope," said Rolland. He added to Mercado, "Steady, you. I can do more damage with this gun than Workin could do with his stiletto."

Roger Rolland had never been more wrong in his life. But at the time he knew it no more than I did.

Mercado said, "Stay where you are, Workin. Rolland, drop that gun," and his voice was steady as a continent. Somehow, all the fear of a moment ago, all the tremulous horror, had dropped from him.

He spoke again. "Stand by, Latham. I may need some help." He advanced a step toward Rolland who raised his weapon so that it was levelled at Mercado's temple. Then Mercado, moving like a mongoose, ducked his head and made the damnedest flying tackle ever made south of the Texan border.

Rolland went to the ground with Mercado on top of him. Workin uttered a cry of alarm and reached again for his knife. Tardily, I decided it was time for me to get into the fray. I laid my hands on the most likely weapon—Workin's shovel.

I swung it like a warclub and nailed Workin on the side of the head. He travelled six feet through the air and landed thuddingly beside the grave.

I picked up Rolland's automatic from between the struggling legs of him and Mercado. I bent and pressed its muzzle against Rolland's head.

I said, "Relax, Mercado. Rolland, get up."

Each did as he was told. "You stay here with the gun and the prisoners," said Mercado. "I'll go up to the house and telephone our friend *el coronel*. I do not think," he added thoughtfully, "that under the circumstances he can claim any reward."

He walked off, a cocky and erect figure in the now brilliant moonlight....

We sat in Mercado's office, a half empty bottle of *habanero* before us. He was in high fettle; I felt good myself.

"A nice piece of work," I told him, "but one point still baffles me."

"I thought I'd cleared up everything."

"No. I want to know why you were in complete panic when Workin held that knife on you; why you were a reckless hero against Rolland with his gun?"

Mercado looked at me as if my stupidity surpassed all understanding. *"Pero, amigo,"* he said, "that knife was jagged, rusty and filthy. Millions of bacteria on that blade." He shuddered.

"Are there no germs on a bullet?"

"Not after it is fired. You see, the tremendous heat of the barrel sterilizes it. There could have been no germs on it after Rolland had fired."

This, I decided, was no longer an eccentricity. It was egregious fanaticism.

I said, "Both of them can kill you."

"Of course. But you are looking only on the pessimistic side. If the bullet fails to kill me I have a nice clean wound. If the knife fails—" He broke off and trembled from head to foot. "Latham," he said, pointing a brown finger at me, "do you know how many bacteria can dwell on the edge of a dirty knife?"

I sighed and filled up my glass. It was a hell of a lot more than you think.

www.ingramcontent.com/pod-product-compliance
Lightning Source LLC
Chambersburg PA
CBHW031105020726
47495CB00007B/2060